By Jeannette Eyerly

A GIRL LIKE ME

A
GIRL
LIKE ME

❀ ❀

Jeannette Eyerly

❀

J. B. LIPPINCOTT COMPANY
Philadelphia   *New York*

The characters in this book are fictitious, and any resemblance they may bear to any persons living or dead is purely coincidental.

ISBN-0-397-30869-8 Tr. Ed.

Copyright © 1966 by Jeannette Eyerly
MEMBER OF THE AUTHORS' LEAGUE OF AMERICA
Printed in the United States of America
Library of Congress Catalog Card Number AC 66-10022

EIGHTH PRINTING

Typography by Tere LoPrete

For Humphry,
the basset who helped me write this book

CONTENTS

PART ONE

I

It was a gift, Robin thought. Some had it and some did not. She was one who didn't. Try as hard as she might, she could no more translate the long silent sentence her friend, Judy Hart, was mouthing to her from the other side of the classroom than if she'd been shut in a dark closet. In sheer frustration, she shook her head to make Judy stop and started copying the Junior English assignment Miss Bird was putting on the blackboard.

The hard little square of folded paper fell with a plop on her desk. Robin recognized the handwriting as that of the girl who sat behind her. Though not very bright, she had got the message.

"Judy says Cass Carter wants you to meet her at her locker after school. Judy didn't get a chance to tell you before class started and she's getting excused early to go to the dentist."

Robin wiggled her fingers over her shoulder in acknowledgment. As she did so she noticed that Judy was already gathering her books together. On her way to the door, Judy paused just long enough to screw up her eyebrows, spread her mouth wide, and transmit a silent postscript to her previous message.

But what, Robin thought, had she said? The words "good luck" were a possibility. Although there were other girls in the senior class who were prettier and more popular than Cass Carter, her shoulder-length red-gold hair was striking and her friendly, outgoing manner had made her many friends.

Robin crossed the first and second fingers of her right hand, locking them so closely that she could feel the hurt. "Please," she said, "let something nice be about to happen." For the past year she had said the words to herself so many times that they had almost passed from wish to prayer. It was funny, but before that she hadn't cared she wasn't dating. Now that she was a junior, a whole world of new and exciting things were going on. Dances, slumber parties, jam sessions. Serious discussions about Civil Rights and capital punishment that she only knew about from snatches of conversation heard around school.

Of course, some things that went on were not good at all. Judy might have said, "Be careful." After all, Cass dated Brew Winfield—Brewster Bailey Winfield III, to be exact—and some of the kids he went around with were pretty fast. Robin smiled with embarrassment at her imagination. There was certainly no danger she'd get involved with Brew Winfield.

Most likely, Judy had simply said "I'll call you." She did call most every night. As Judy said, "There's only one of you at your house and there are five of us kids. It's easier to make a call to the Kremlin than it is to get through to the Harts'."

But whatever Judy's message, now there was no way for Robin to find out. The teacher had turned and was facing the class. With her humorous gray-blue eyes upon them there would be no more note passing. Robin was still wondering what Cass wanted to see her about when the last bell rang.

Instead of turning right at the next intersection of corridors which would have led to her own locker almost a half block away, Robin turned left.

Judy's locker was next door to Cass Carter's. Once when Cass had left her key at home, she'd borrowed Judy's gym shoes. That was how the two had become acquainted. Although they didn't see each other any place but school, Judy liked her.

Two girls and a tall good-looking boy stood around

Cass's open locker. All were seniors Robin knew only by sight. Brew Winfield was not there.

Robin stood outside the circle waiting for Cass to speak. She did, a second later. "Oh, hi!" she smiled. "Just a minute, until I get loose from the mob." She shook her head at the boy who had moved in closer. "Sorry, but Brew would kill me if he found out I let you drive me home. And probably kill you, too, in the bargain."

The boy said, "Ha!" derisively, but he stepped back a pace as a friend coming down the hall took his arm. "Don't waste your time on her. She's signed, sealed, and delivered."

As the boys moved away, Cass whispered something Robin could not hear to the girls then shut her locker door with a bang.

"Thanks for waiting," she said, as she came toward Robin. "But I didn't want to talk to you in front of all those kids."

Her smile was so friendly, her manner so easy that Robin accepted at once when Cass suggested they go across the street to the drugstore to have a Coke. It proved, however, to be a poor place to talk. Cass was on the committee for the Senior Frolics and kids kept coming by with questions and advice. Robin was about ready to expire from curiosity when Cass said, "Honestly! This place is as bad as that street corner cafe in Paris. What do they call it—the Rue de la Paix? They say if a person sits there long enough the whole world passes by."

As Cass spoke, she gave Robin such a curious, half-appraising look that Robin's eyes fell.

A little apologetically Cass looked away. "It's funny, but I don't think a girl ever looks at another girl the way a boy does. You really are every bit as pretty as Randy Griffin said you were."

"Me?" Robin said vapidly. "Randy Griffin. I . . . I don't think I know him."

"I don't know him very well myself. He's Brew's friend, really. They knew each other when Brew went to George Washington High."

Not knowing where the conversation might be leading, Robin managed only a diffident little "oh."

"Well, anyway," Cass went on, "I'd better get to the point. The other day Brew didn't have his car so Randy came by school to pick up Brew and me and drive us home. Just as we were leaving the parking lot, we saw you and Judy Hart crossing the street ahead of us. Randy almost flipped. 'Wow!' he said. 'Look at that queen! She's for me!' "

Robin stared. "Who . . . who did he mean?"

Cass laughed. "Well, he didn't mean Judy. She's a nice girl and I like her. But she's not Randy Griffin's type."

"What . . . what kind is his type?"

"You are, I guess," Cass said. "That's what I wanted to see you about. When Randy found out I knew you, he asked me to fix him up with you. For Saturday night, if you're not busy. Don't know what we'll do. But something fun."

Robin stared down at the table before her. "I don't know what to say."

The silence that had preceded Robin's words were so awkward that Cass looked curious. "Don't you like blind dates?"

"I don't know." Robin raised embarrassed eyes to Cass's face. "I never had one."

Cass laughed. "There are some I wish I hadn't had. Sometimes, they're dreadful. I can't promise you what Randy is like on a date—he's different, sort of—but Brew thinks he's great. And you know what I think of Brew."

Cass's face grew soft and vulnerable-looking as she mentioned Brew's name. Robin could not help noticing and it made her feel a little twinge around her own heart. How would it feel, she wondered, to care so much about a boy?

"Brew had to pick his mother up right after school and drive her downtown because she had something wrong with her car," Cass continued, "otherwise he'd have come along to help convince you. But, of course, if you really don't want to go . . ."

Robin felt a moment of panic. "It's not that . . ." She faltered and stopped. She remembered the feeling she had had as a child when a large red balloon, helium-filled, slipped from her fingers almost the moment she touched it and disappeared from sight. Something like that was about to happen again. The thing she wanted most was about to slip through her fingers because she dared not tell Cass Carter that before she could say "yes" she would have to ask her mother! There was a reason she had to ask, of course, and as bothersome as it was, *she* understood it, but would Cass?

Then suddenly, almost unbelievably, Cass was solving everything. "Would it help, maybe, if I went with you? If your parents are like mine—my dad, particularly— they practically want a boy's fingerprints before they'll let you go out with him. And since you don't know Randy at all . . ."

"Would you really?" Robin could not quite contain herself. "I'm sure my mother would say yes if you came with me."

Cass looked up at the clock on the wall. "Four thirty. If you don't live too far, I guess there's time. I've got to get home, though, before my father leaves for work. He's on the night shift now."

The March wind did its best to slow them down. Robin raised her chin from the protection of her warm jacket. "Just another block." Cass with her fair skin looked half frozen.

Turning the corner on Putnam Avenue, the wind was broken by the heavy planting on the deep, wide lawns which, even with patches of snow upon them, showed signs of care. "That's our house. The rambly white one with the yellow shutters. The big orange, furry thing on the porch is Carrie Chapman, our cat. And most important, that Volksie in the drive is my mother's. Means she's home."

The front door was unlocked and as the girls stepped inside Robin yoo-hooed. An answering yoo-hoo seemed to come from the bowels of the house. "She's in the basement," Robin said, "developing pictures. She's a photographer. Birds. Though she does take pictures of other things, mainly me." She grimaced. "I guess I'm really her favorite subject."

Robin crossed the big, pleasantly cluttered living room toward the back of the house. "I'll see if she's coming up or if she wants us to come down."

Robin was back a minute later. "I told her you were here. She's coming up. She said she wouldn't want to meet anyone whose opinion she valued to step foot into our basement. It's a regular Grendel's lair."

"You must excuse the way I look," Mrs. James said. "I've been down in that dreadful place for hours."

Mrs. James had appeared almost immediately behind Robin, and as she walked toward Cass with her right hand outstretched, the other hand rather ineffectually tried to tuck in a strand of silver-threaded dark hair that had escaped from a softly-piled topknot on her handsome head. "You're Cass," she said. "I'd have known who you were even if Robin hadn't said you were here. I saw you in *South Pacific* when you gave it at school and thought you every bit as good as Mary Martin!"

"Thank you, Mrs. James. You're nice to say so. It was

a terribly ambitious thing for a bunch of high school kids to attempt. I think all the credit goes to Mr. Gartner who directed it. He lost twenty pounds during rehearsal! And I, who would have given anything to lose even one, gained three. Robin, the lucky thing, is just right the way she is—and I know someone else who thinks so, too."

This was her cue, Robin knew, but before she could say a word Cass smiled in her direction. "I'll tell your mother about Randy, if you like. It might be pretty embarrassing for you to repeat all those compliments." Not waiting for Robin's euphoric nod, she bubbled on. "You see, there's this boy. His name is Randy Griffin. He's a friend of Brewster Winfield, the boy I go with. Well, the other day when Brew and I were with him, he spotted Robin. Well, he flipped. And when he found out I knew who she was—Judy Hart lockers right next to me and I'd seen them together loads of times—Randy asked me if I'd ask Robin if she'd go out with him on Saturday night. There's a teen hop at the Youth Center. We might go to that, or a movie. We'll have twice as much fun if we can double."

Robin held on tight, closed her eyes and when she opened them her mother was smiling. "I think it would be nice for Robin to go," Mrs. James said. "I'm assuming, of course, that she wants to."

Robin gave a little caper then caught her mother in a strangling hug, not caring in the least if Cass thought her

: 23 :

juvenile. "Now can I take Cass home in the car after she came all this way with me? I'll be terribly careful. I promise."

"I don't know why not. But remember the traffic will be heavy this hour of the evening. And don't linger."

"She always tells me not to linger," Robin said as she backed the car out of the driveway. "But at least she didn't remind me that I've only had my license for a month. I got it the very day I was sixteen. Now you tell me which way to go."

The traffic was heavy as Mrs. James had predicted and although Robin was really rather proud of her driving skill she was glad that Cass kept up a light pleasant chatter that demanded little from her as she wound her way onto the freeway that bisected the city. Some blocks later, at the point Cass indicated, she successfully exited, coming down and around onto a street of big old houses. Before the freeway came and the city moved on, they had been fine homes. Thin skins of ice lay in patches in their bare front yards. Across the street, a small boy was bent under the weight of a huge canvas bag filled with newspapers.

Cass, who had grown quiet, laughed softly. "That's my brother, Louis. After I go home and check in, I'll come back and help him deliver."

"I'd help you," Robin said promptly, "if I hadn't promised my mother not to linger."

Cass laughed. "Don't you dare!" She began gathering

her books together. "It's the first house in the next block. But you can drop me right here."

"Indeed, not! I'm going to bring you home in style." With a flourish, Robin turned in the drive.

Cass got out. Her face looked pale in the waning light. "Thanks for the ride. Tonight if Brew calls I'll tell him the good news and he can tell Randy. I expect you'll hear from him before Saturday."

"Oh, good," Robin said, though she hardly thought it was good at all. Dancing was one thing, and about that she felt secure, but what one said over the telephone to a boy one had never seen and who was "different," she had no idea.

She watched as Cass ran toward her house. The largest on the block it still retained elements of grandeur—ornate latticework on the porch, a diamond-shaped window of stained glass, a porte-cochere.

As Cass turned to wave, the front door opened. A strongly-built man in a too-tight T shirt seemed to fill it.

Before the car door swung shut, Robin could not help but hear. She wished she had left Cass at the curb.

"Don't 'hello, Daddy' me," he said gruffly. "You're late. Get on in the house and help your mother with the kids."

2

"Daddy called while you were taking Cass home to say he wouldn't be home for dinner," Mrs. James said. "And, for once, I'm almost glad. It will give me a chance to finish developing the pictures I took yesterday of the cedar waxwings polishing off the last of the crabapples. So be an angel and fix us any old thing to eat. And I'll go back downstairs. O.K.?"

"I'll fix my specialty," Robin said promptly. "But poor Daddy! What's keeping him?"

"Some orthoptera he's been watching for days are about to hatch. Wild horses couldn't drag him away."

"They're neat. I saw them last Saturday when I was helping at the lab."

Mrs. James was already fading toward the basement door. Her mind, Robin thought, was already in her dark room. Robin's father said, that had she wanted, she could have become as famous a bird photographer as Eliot Porter and traveled the world over taking pictures of sulphur-crested cockatoos, lorikeets, and toucans. "Instead, she married a poor but honest entomologist," he'd say, "and while I don't know how *she* feels, *I've* never regretted it for a minute."

Robin got out ground beef, kidney beans, and other ingredients for her specialty which in the long ago had been known as chili. But even when it was bubbling in the big yellow Dansk pot and the warm spicy smell brought Mrs. James up the stairs, Robin did not feel hungry. Grateful that her mother did not press her to eat, in a burst of gratitude she volunteered to do the dishes. The offer, of course, was not purely unselfish. If Randy should call, it would be less gruesome if she could talk to him without anyone at all listening.

The telephone, however, refused to cooperate and sat there in stony silence as Robin tried to do her homework. There was so much else to think about—a date on Saturday night with a boy who, until that afternoon, she did not even know existed! In addition, there was Cass, herself. From seeing her at school it was hard for Robin to believe that Cass lived on such a sad run-down street.

Robin's mother, though, had not been surprised. Just interested. "Cass is well-liked not because she drives her own car, gives big parties or has socially prominent parents, but because she is a nice person." Robin nodded to herself. Her mother had a good way of making points— not preachy, but still in a way one would remember. It even explained the seemingly un-Cass-like business of helping her little brother deliver papers. It was something that a nice person like Cass *would* do.

At nine thirty her mother came up from her dark room carrying a sheaf of pictures and a few minutes later, the headlights of Mr. James' car beamed in the driveway.

Robin leaped up, glad of the diversion. "Did they hatch?"

Mr. James eyes, dark and deep-set, crinkled cheerfully as he shrugged out of his hairy old tweed topcoat. "Thousands and thousands of fine, fat bouncing baby grasshoppers. Left to their own devices they could munch their way clear across the country. Which reminds me that somehow I forgot to get anything to eat, myself." He put on his pitiful, hungry look. "You don't suppose . . ."

"There's lots of 'specialty' left," Mrs. James said. "It's not your favorite food, I know, but it will take just a minute to warm it up."

The phone rang as they walked arm in arm to the kitchen.

Robin silenced it on its very first bleat. Her breathless

"hello" was followed by a little giggle of relief. "Oh, Judy. I didn't think it was going to be you."

"For Heaven's sake," Judy replied with some asperity. "Who did you think it was going to be—some movie star?"

"No, but I did think it might be a boy. That was what Cass Carter wanted to see me about."

"And that's why I called. To find out what happened. Start at the beginning and tell me everything."

Although Robin would have liked nothing more than to relay word for word everything that Cass said, she couldn't bring herself to do it. That part where Randy had said, "Wow! What a queen! She's for me!" sounded too vain to tell your best friend who was ten pounds too fat and whose complexion had not yet straightened out.

Even before Judy called, Robin had decided to pare the account down to its bare essentials.

As she talked, Judy kept interrupting with little squeals of genuine delight. It wasn't until Robin said, "He's Brew's friend really, and his name is Randy Griffin," that a strange silence fell at the other end of the line. "Cass says he's awfully cute," Robin concluded a little lamely. "And Randy thinks I'm just his type."

"Did you ever stop to think that maybe Randy Griffin isn't *your* type?"

"What . . . what do you mean?" Robin cast a quick glance over her shoulder at her parents who had come back in the living room and stood looking at the newly developed pictures Mrs. James had spread out on the harvest table.

"Just that. I mean that maybe he isn't your type." Judy's blunt voice was reverberating much too loudly though Robin held the receiver so tightly against her ear that it hurt.

"After all," Judy went on, "what do you know about him? What's 'cute'? What's important, and you know it as well as I do, Robin James, is 'Is he nice?'"

Robin forced an unreal laugh. "Honestly, Judy! I'll let you know later. About everything. But now I've got to go. Daddy just got home and he wants to use the phone."

The lie was so small and so white it should not have stirred the surface of her conscience. Yet something did. For a long time after she went to bed she lay awake. What, she wondered, had come over Judy? Why had her attitude, which had at first been so pleased, turned so critical?

Although Judy had a lot of friends, both boys and girls, she didn't date at all. Could she possibly be—jealous? Robin allowed the traitorous thought barely to cross her mind before she erased it. It was impossible. Judy was her best friend. They had known each other since they had first stared, then smiled at each other across the circle of little chairs in kindergarten.

If Judy had ever been jealous of her, it happened on a day not too long after that—the day she'd forgotten to bring something to "show" for "show and tell" time. To make up for the lack, she'd told the best thing she knew: how her mommy and daddy, lonely for a baby, had to look and look before they found her, and had adopted her for their very own. "I was the prettiest little baby," she'd concluded placidly, "they'd ever had at the Child Jesus Home."

Even now, after all these years, Robin could barely suppress a giggle at what happened next. Old practical Judy had not believed her! Planting her fat legs firmly, Judy had said stubbornly, "If you're 'dopted, I'm 'dopted." In the end, to prove her story, Robin had taken Judy home at recess where Robin's mother had smilingly said that it was true. Every word.

It was easier to believe that Judy was . . . well, a Communist, than that she was jealous.

In all likelihood, Judy had not been nearly as disapproving as she sounded. After all, she had only asked the obvious question, "Is he nice?" And I'll find that out Saturday night, Robin thought firmly. She turned her pillow over to cool her hot cheek, adding mentally, "And even if he *isn't* nice, why should Judy be in such a stew? I'm only going to a dance with Randy Griffin. I'm not going to marry him."

"Robin, it's Sam."
Robin heard her mother's voice coming faintly through the eiderdown puff, slowly opened her eyes. "Sam?"

"Sam. He's downstairs."

Robin peered at the clock on the bedside table and assured that in spite of the gray March weather outside that it was really morning, sat up. "Sam Drew? What's he downstairs for? What does he want before a person is out of bed or has had her breakfast?"

"You're not really awake yet or you wouldn't ask. You know that Sam, at any hour, is a man of very few words."

Robin giggled. Her mother could always make her laugh, even when she was not in the mood for it at all.

"I was getting Daddy's breakfast," Mrs. James went on, "when I saw Sam at the back door. I asked him to come in. And assuming that he had not come to see Daddy or me, I told him you weren't up yet but that I was going to wake you in a minute. This seemed to please him. Anyway, he came in and sat down at the kitchen table. Right now, he's having a second breakfast while waiting for you to appear."

"Oh, well." Robin leaped out of bed. It really was getting late. "Tell him I'll be down in a shake. No, don't. But I will be down."

Robin stared unseeingly into her closet, her mind only partially occupied with what to wear. The rest of her mind was dealing with Sam. Her father called him "Silent Sam." "He's polite enough," he once said, "but I swear it's easier to work up conversation with a cigar-store Indian than it is with Sam Drew."

"He talks to me," she countered, feeling that Sam

while not talkative, was being a bit maligned. In all truth, however, months passed before she could say that they were really communicating.

It had all begun the summer before when her mother found the neatly-typed card stuck in the front screen door. "Look!" she cried. "Someone to *mow!* I can't stand it!" She thrust the card toward Robin and pretended to swoon.

S. M. DREW
Yardman-Experienced
No Job Too Large
No Job too Small
Phone answered
Day Or Night
109–2685

The yardman had turned out to be Sam. Now they were friends. They had even had a few dates. None of them had been very exciting. Once, last summer they had gone to the State Fair where Sam's ability to throw baseballs and shoot pistols at moving objects resulted in a dreadful array of plastic Kewpie dolls with hula skirts of chicken feathers, dyed red and green, and sleazy stuffed animals being thrust into her unwilling arms. The stuffed animals she had given to the neighborhood children. The dolls she had stealthily burned, the feathers making the most dreadful smell.

A Girl Like Me

Another time they had gone to a masquerade party. She had really looked forward to it and had spent hours on her Alice in Wonderland costume. When Sam, who was keeping his costume a secret, appeared at the front door dressed as an alligator, wearing a most realistic head of papier-mâché and carrying his long green stuffed tail over his arm, she had not known whether to laugh or cry. That was not the worst. Getting in the car—his mother was driving—he slammed the door on his tail which resulted in cries of anguish that could not have been more real if the hurt had been truly physical. By the time the judging of the costumes took place and Sam was able to remove his "head" he was in such a state of near suffocation that he had to lie down. Neither he nor she had won a prize.

Robin sighed as she took a long-sleeved white blouse and green corduroy jumper from the closet. The jumper, if not the color of her eyes, did make them seem more green than blue. She brushed her dark, straight bangs, sleek as sable until they barely touched her eyebrows. The rest of her hair fell just as straight and sleek to her shoulders. It looked nice and it felt nice. Now that it was this long she was glad that she had let it grow. The old way she'd worn her hair she might not have been Randy's type of girl at all. She searched her face for a faint pink spot or a small hard lump that might presage a pimple that would erupt in all of its horridness by Saturday night. Fortunately, there was none and after deciding against lipstick—Sam would not notice one way or the other—she made her bed in a rather slapdash fashion and went downstairs.

Sam got to his feet when she came in the kitchen, if not straightening up completely he did manage to unfold.

She said, "Hi!" eyeing Sam's sweet roll, a rather large bite of which was occupying him at the moment.

Sam's "Hi" was bready.

Robin drank her orange juice which was already on the table, then got herself two sweet rolls from the warming oven.

Her mother was not in sight.

His roll gone, Sam finished a half glass of milk at a swallow. "Well," he said, "I've got it." He looked enormously pleased with himself.

In fact, Robin thought, that if head and hands and feet were not quite so large he would be quite a handsome boy. As it was, he looked scrubbed and healthy and his smile was awfully nice.

Robin buttered her roll. "Got what?"

"Dad's car. It's outside."

Robin put down her roll, stared at Sam with so vague an expression that he laughed.

"Don't you remember? Dad promised me I could have the car if he decided to go to that refresher course in Boston this week end. Well, he decided. Left this morning and I've his car. Full of gas and ready to go. I've got work after school today and tomorrow but on Saturday we'll do something for sure."

It was a long speech for Sam and his voice had grown a little husky as his big square hand moved across the blue and white checked tablecloth towards hers. It was a nice hand, with blunt clean fingernails and fine gold hair on the back that glinted in the sunshine streaming in through the window behind them.

Uneasily, Robin drew her hand away. Walking home from a movie one Sunday afternoon an age ago, she did remember hearing Sam say that if his dad decided to go to Boston for some kind of a refresher course the last week end in March that he could have the car. But that was all. He hadn't asked her for a date. If he had, she'd remember that—unless, accidentally, her mind, as it so often was with Sam, was somewhere else.

"You didn't *forget*, did you, Rob?" Sam's voice was unbelieving.

"You didn't ask me." Cross with Sam and cross with herself, she tore the last of her roll to shreds, muddled the pile with her forefinger, slowly raised her eyes. "Now I'm afraid I've got other plans."

"Well, how do you like that?" Sam muttered. His face had grown quite red.

The question had been addressed to an imaginary grievance committee, Robin decided, and required no answer. Moreover, from the corner of her eye she could see he was crumbling.

"You could break it if you wanted," Sam said, but there was no conviction in his voice.

Robin shook her head, glad to be spared a further answer as her mother came back into the kitchen.

"I hate to interrupt," Mrs. James said briskly, "but if that clock on the stove is right, school begins in just fourteen minutes."

3

"Will, dear, will you please quit pacing?"

"I'm not pacing," Robin's father replied with dignity.

He did, however, Robin noticed, sit down. From her observation post—the window seat in the darkened dining room—she not only had a view of the living room where her parents sat, but more importantly, the street in front of the house. The porch lights were on, also the O'Leary-like lamp post that stood near the entrance to the drive. In one direction, she could see clear to the corner.

The headlights of a car beamed toward her, seemed

to slow in front of her house, then moved on. Robin sighed. She wished Cass and Brew and Randy would come.

Someone else wished so, too.

"When I was a young man and went out with a girl, we at least got started at a decent hour. Will James looked at his watch. "Nine fifteen. The evening's half over."

"Oh, Will!" her mother answered with a little laugh. "Times change, you know. They'll be here any minute now, anyway. You'll see."

Robin could hear the sounds her father made as he filled his pipe. The scratch of the match, the little wheezes the pipe made as he sucked in. Then there was silence so deep that Robin could hear her heart plopping against her ribs. Again she sighed. The three days she'd been waiting for the date with Randy, and which should have been happy days, had not been happy at all.

In the first place, Randy had not called. Nor had Judy Hart helped the situation. Although insisting that she didn't know a single bad thing about Randy, she had managed to look annoyingly wise when Robin had questioned her at school.

Not until the day before when she was on the verge of tears did Judy admit that her low opinion of Randy Griffin was simply the result of ESP.

"That stands for Extra-Sensory Perception," Judy said. "And it means you absolutely know something for sure when you haven't any real facts. What I do know is that Randy is a friend of Brew Winfield. I can't stand Brew Winfield. One pill . . . two pills. And there you are—ESP."

Although Judy, who planned to be a psychiatrist, was a mine of information on such subjects as ESP, in this case, Robin thought, the evidence against Randy seemed flimsy. But the business of Sam Drew was something else again. She did not need Judy Hart to tell her—though Judy did, at length—that if a date was to be broken it should be broken with Randy Griffin. To make matters worse, Sam was stiff and unforgiving. All the way to school the morning he'd stopped by with the car, he'd maintained a silence so complete that it made the old silent Sam seem garrulous by comparison. She'd only seen him once since and that had been at school. He'd passed her in the corridor like a large iceberg on its way to the sea.

Robin heard the low rumble of the car before it turned the corner. Sounding rather like the purring of an enormous and not too friendly cat, it came down the street. Another car was behind it, which was strange. She slid off the window seat, noticing as she did so that her father was already on his feet and prowling toward the window.

"Sit down, Daddy," Robin said. "I'll go."

"*I'll* go," said her father.

Behind his back, Robin cast a despairing look at her

mother who did not return it in kind as she had hoped. Instead, it only repeated what she'd whispered earlier when Robin's father was not listening, "I've soothed him the best I could, but it *is* getting late to be starting out on a date with a boy you don't know, and with no very clear idea of where you are going."

Robin put on her coat, picked up gloves and purse and gave her mother's hand a forgiving squeeze. After all, she could hardly expect—or want—her parents to disappear into the woodwork. It would be dreadful to have a mother and father who didn't care who you went out with or what time you got home.

Outside in the hall she could hear her father's growly-deep but still pleasant voice saying, "I'm Robin's father. Won't you please all step inside?"

For a moment, Robin felt herself suspended in time and space as she stared at the little tableau now standing just inside the living room. Cass, her color high, had a Kelly green scarf tied over her bright red-gold hair. Brew stood beside her in a protective but yet possessive way, one hand on her shoulder, his trench coat belted spy-style around his waist. Randy stood a step behind. He was not tall—but, of course, Cass had not said he was—and he had a sturdy, muscular build. His eyes were dark, deep-set and intense; his mouth mobile and insolent. Curly, chestnut-colored hair seemed to fit his head like a thick furry cap. She had not thought he would look that way at all.

Cass was saying, "Mrs. James, this is my friend, Brewster Winfield; and Mr. James, Brew Winfield; Mrs. James, this is Randy Griffin; Mr. James, Randy Griffin." So like a well-trained parrot had she performed the introductions, not pausing to spew out her breath in a little "Whew!" until she had ended with "and Robin, this is Randy" that even Will James who, it seemed to Robin, was viewing Randy with disfavor, finally smiled.

"Don't worry about Robin," Brew said heartily. He gave Robin's father an unwanted hand-shake. "Right, Randy?"

"Right, sir." Randy stepped forward, repeated the hand-shaking act and after a chorus of "goodnight, sirs," and "goodnight, Mrs. James's" the three of them—Cass, Brew, and Randy, with Robin somewhere in the middle—moved like a well-oiled piece of machinery out to the front porch and into the night.

"How was that for the Old Statue of Liberty play?" Brew pounded Randy delightedly on the back.

Randy laughed. "Right! Get 'em out of the house in a hurry and avoid the third degree."

They moved down the sidewalk, Cass shivering in a coat that seemed too thin for the sharp March air.

Randy took Robin's hand and held it so tightly that she would have had to tussle had she wished to pull it away. He made a quarter-turn toward Brew who was a step behind. "See you there, O.K.?"

Robin, who had not spoken since the front door of her house had closed behind her, let out a startled

PART ONE: *Robin*

squeak. "Aren't we going to go together? Aren't we going to double?"

"We'll double when we get there," Cass interposed. "We're really doubling—just not going in the same car. It's better this way, in case someone wants to go home earlier..."

"Or stay out later." Brew finished the sentence with a jab at Randy's ribs.

Robin looked over her shoulder. The porch light was still on. "Maybe we'd better be going." Although splitting up, going in two cars was an arrangement that did not please her, it would please her parents even less. Nor would it be an arrangement that was easy to explain. Wondering if Cass had known all along they would not really be doubling, she allowed Randy to settle her in the front seat of the car. A moment later he had slipped in beside her. As the car roared away from the curb he pulled her, with a strong muscular arm, from her stiffly upright position in the middle of her half of the front seat so that she slid against him. His eyes glinted mischievously in the reflected light from the dash.

"That's better, isn't it?"

"Better than what?" Robin's voice was cross and she did not care. This cave-man approach on top of everything else was really too much. She pulled herself straight and slid back to her half of the seat.

Randy laughed, not seeming to mind at all. He flipped a switch on the instrument panel and twisted the dial until he found music that seemed to suit him. To her

:31:

surprise, it was a slow-moving piece with a haunting melody. His grin was impish. "Maybe this will put you in a better mood."

Robin cast a sidewise glance in his direction. After all, the whole evening lay ahead of them. The sky, which had been filled all day with scudding clouds, was now clear and a moon rose high and handsome above them.

Randy seemed to read her mind. "Maybe we could compromise," he said. "Maybe divide the distance?"

Robin slid three inches closer. After all, what could you do with a boy like that?

It was lovely in the car. Sometimes Randy sang softly along with the orchestra. His voice, smooth and at the same time husky, made little prickles come along her spine. Behind and all around them she could hear the motor throbbing like a great mechanical heart.

"Buick Special," Randy said. "Five years old but as good as the day it came off the line. In eighteen months, three weeks, and five days it will be all mine."

"It isn't your *father's*?"

Although the question, to Robin, seemed a natural one, Randy laughed inordinately. "My old man drive a car like this? He doesn't drive any car. But that's his tough luck, not mine. You got to learn to play the game, figure the angles; when you see what you want, you got to take it. That's why I got this car. It's my type." Randy's voice grew soft. "When I saw it, I said 'Hello, baby, you're for me.'"

The words, although the context was familiar, were

pushed to the back of her mind. "I managed the down payment, now all I got to do is figure out how to keep up the payments until fall. Fellow I know is going to give me a real job then. On the road."

"You're—not going to college?"

"College!" Randy laughed humorlessly. "If somebody doesn't give me a break, I'm not even going to graduate from high school." He shrugged. "But who cares? It's not a criminal offense."

"I didn't mean that. I meant that kids ought to try to go college if they can."

"Not this kid. Right now, I've got everything I need." His voice had become soft and silky-smooth. "I've got me a car. And I've got me something else, too—a girl."

Robin felt goose bumps rise as his lips brushed against her cheek. So early in the evening the turn this conversation was taking would not do at all! Besides, she did not even know where they were going. "See you there," Brew had said. But where was *there*? Ever since they got in the car they had seemed to be riding aimlessly around. She was sure that they had driven past one corner several times.

"Where is this place we're going?" Not wishing to seem concerned, Robin asked the question with forced brightness. The clock on the dashboard said it was ten o'clock.

"Nowhere special," Randy said. He seemed a bit surprised.

"But how will we ever meet Cass and Brew? How are

they ever going to meet *us*?" Let Randy think her unsophisticated if he wanted, now she really had to know.

Randy laughed tolerantly. "Don't worry, baby. We'll find them. There are lots of places kids hang out. Nobody really knows in advance where most of the kids will be. It's a game, kind of. I'm betting on Dinty's. It's a new place out in Rosedale."

Robin knew Rosedale. A shopping center in the northwestern part of the city. "Dinty's" did not mean a thing.

"I'll say it's Dinty's," Randy crowed after they had ridden around perhaps five minutes more. "Look at that mob! The joint is jumping tonight."

Robin looked, her worry forgotten in a glow of excitement. So many cars! So many kids! Where had they all come from? Yet Dinty's, itself, wasn't much. A small, garishly painted structure set in a giant arch of twisting and flashing neon lights that spelled the name. A parking area that seemed to stretch a quarter of a block in each direction was filled to the brim with cars. In spite of herself, Robin felt her pulses tingling as lights flashed, automobile horns blared, and tires squealed. Over everything there was the heavy odor of hot grease and cooking hamburgers.

Randy swung the car into the parking area, expertly pulling into a space just vacated by a Model T Ford so filled with kids that for a moment Robin had the impression that an animated cartoon had come to life.

"It's going to be a 'go' night," Randy said approvingly. "Dinty's is a new place, but I thought it would catch on." He looked around. "Well, what do you say I go on a still hunt for Cass and Brew? Then we can get something to eat."

He did not wait for an answer but got out, turning once to wave as he wound his way among the parked cars. Although many were occupied, there also seemed to be considerable milling about accompanied by rather loud laughter and girls' high-pitched laughter. Robin wished Randy had asked her to go with him. She stared straight ahead as she saw a boy coming toward her. He lurched as he reached the car, slopping beer from the can he held in his hand. "Wh' kin' a guy you got, leavin' pre'y li'l thing like you allalone ina car?"

Robin snapped the lock on the door before the boy, uncoordinated as he was, could turn the handle. As quickly, she locked herself in on the other side. She was only half angry and not at all afraid. It was a scene, she thought, that F. Scott Fitzgerald would have liked! Just one little blast from the horn on Randy's car—it sounded rather like an angry "Mooo" and like no other horn she had ever heard—and he would come running. Nevertheless, she kept the doors locked until she saw him coming. Brew and Cass were not with him but he did not seem at all perturbed. "No sign of 'em," he said, cheerfully. "We'll try across the street."

"What's across the street?" Robin asked, curiously. "It looks to me as if everything is closed." The drugstore, catercorner from Dinty's had been dark when they arrived. And the filling station opposite had closed while Randy was away looking for Cass and Brew. That left only the supermarket on the other corner. Low and sprawling, the building was an island in an acre of concrete.

As Randy turned in the nearest entrance, Robin was glad she had asked no more questions. In the beams from their car's headlights, she could not see what had been invisible before. Cars. Dozens of them. Hundreds. Shocked, yet at the same time curious she did not know whether to stare or to turn her eyes away.

Randy was unconcerned. "Whoever first thought of bringing his girl over here to make out deserves a medal. Of course, if it's privacy you want it's hardly the place. But kids have got to go somewhere. Safer than a country road or a park where somebody's apt to mug you. Better, though, than sitting out in front of your girl's house where her old man can keep his eye on you."

A car tootled softly behind them. Randy slowed, laughing. "Looks as if they're following *us*." He rolled down the window on his side, beckoned for Brew to drive along side.

Robin could see Brew's face in the glow from the dash. "You coming with us or are we coming with you?"

"You ride with us," Randy said after a little pause that seemed to have contained a silent interchange of information. "We'll go back over to Dinty's and get something to eat. By then, maybe something will have started cooking."

Although Brew continued expansive, Cass was quiet as the two got in the back seat of Randy's car and drove back across the street to Dinty's. They again found a place to park. Even after the boys went off together to get hamburgers, French fries and malts all around, Cass sat silently with her head lying back against the seat.

"Is something the matter?" Robin felt uneasy. If something was, it would be one more thing gone wrong in an already strange evening. "Did—did you and Brew have a fight?"

"I don't want to talk about it," Cass said in a small muffled voice. Then, as if ashamed of herself, sat up and leaned forward impulsively. "You mustn't mind me. Please, please forget it?"

"Of course," Robin said. She was only too glad to.

"I didn't suggest it, for crying out loud," Brew said. "Pris Gosling did. She said her folks suddenly decided to go out, so she just drove over here to round up some of the gang and have a party, herself. She was inside getting stuff to eat when Randy and I walked in. So she asked us to come."

"I hope you explained to her that you had a date," Cass said in a small contained voice. "And that you made it clear that Randy had one, too."

"Don't be a stupe. Of course, I did." Brew's voice was loud and a little rough.

"Oh, well. I guess it's all right with me, if Randy and Robin want to."

"Why not?" Randy said. He had put the sack of French fries that had been between them on the seat on the little ledge above the dashboard. Now he sat so close to Robin that their arms and legs touched as either reached for a potato or for their big paper container of malted milk.

Robin knew they were all looking at her. What could she say? That with Pris Gosling's parents away from home, that she didn't think it was a good idea? But on the other hand, what would she tell *her* parents about the evening? Tell them they hadn't gone anyplace or done anything except ride around?

"Maybe we could go for a little while," she said.

When their food was gone, Randy finishing what Robin could not eat, they took off for Pris Gosling's house. Both boys knew where she lived. That Brew knew did not seem to please Cass at all and several attempts to get her into the conversation got nowhere. The two boys, however, maintained a steady stream of talk. Brew's mostly concerned kids at school—kids Robin knew only by name. Biz Dudevant, he said, with a loud horsey laugh, had a collection of over a hundred street signs in his basement. His mother made him get rid of them, though, and he'd taken the whole works to the

City Dump. There, just as he was unloading, who should he run into but a squad car with two cops in it. "Biz's dad got him off, though," Brew added easily. "Knows the judge."

"I don't think that's right!" Without thinking, Robin had blurted out the words, leaving a wake of startled silence.

Randy voided it with a tolerant laugh. "Wouldn't you do the same? I mean, if you got in some kind of trouble and you had a big-shot dad, wouldn't you have him get you out of it, if he could?"

"No! I mean, I don't know. I don't think so, anyway...."

Cass broke in almost fiercely from the back seat. "Don't try to mix her up with all your double-talk! She's right. It was wrong for his father to do that, and you know it!"

"Now look who's talking!" Brew scoffed. "Another county heard from."

"Oh, let's skip it," Randy said, still amiable. "O.K.?"

Pris lived not too far from Robin but in an all new neighborhood. The house was ranch type and very like its neighbors, but there was no doubt that at one a party was going on. There were several cars parked in the drive. Lights streamed from the windows and when the front door opened to admit a new arrival, the heavy pulsing rhythm of stereophonic music poured forth.

Cass was out of the car almost before it stopped, pulling Brew along. Her mood seemed to have changed remarkably. "Come on," she cried with a gay toss of her head. "I want to dance. But not to that loudy thumpy stuff. Something slow and dreamy."

Randy pressed Robin's hand. "That suits me, too."

They piled their wraps on a settee in the large front hall that already held a half dozen or so coats and an assortment of gloves and scarves. A little uneasily, Robin looked about. The living room was empty. The record on the phonograph, however, had been changed and at the end of the house in a room Robin took to be the family room, she could see a couple dancing so close together that they seemed to have but a single shape. Although the light was dim, she could see that it was Cass and Brew moving dreamily about.

As Robin and Randy stood there, a couple neither had noticed arose from a sofa in a darkened corner. The girl, slender, with a small piquant face and abused blonde hair came toward them. "Didn't see you come in," she said, "but make yourselves at home." She gave her head an airy little toss. "There's beer in the refrigerator, until it runs out, but I'm afraid my dad's got all the hard stuff under lock and key. There's also some pizza and potato chips and I don't know what all on the counter in the kitchen. That's where I'm headed now. Come on, Biz."

Not until Randy's arm was around her and they had gone on into the darkened family room, did it occur to Robin that Randy had not introduced her to Pris Gosling. But the oversight, if it was that, and not ignorance, was soon forgotten. Forgotten, too, was the shock she'd had at learning that Pris Gosling's date was undoubtedly the Biz Dudevant who had stolen all the street signs. Now all she could think of was Randy. They were standing so very close together, scarcely moving. It could scarcely be called dancing. It was . . . She tried to pull herself away from him but Randy's arm drew her closer still.

"I . . . I want to dance," she said.

Randy laughed softly. "Are you sure?"

"I'm sure."

They started moving in time to the music but it was like being in a dream. Later, when Randy's face, so very near, turned and their lips touched, she thought that she might faint. "No," she said. "Please . . . you mustn't." Almost wildly she looked about her. The other dancers had left. They were alone. The phonograph in the corner of the room was silent.

"One more?" Randy's voice was husky. "Please?"

Robin shook her head. Out of the circle of his arms, the magic circle where she seemed to have no will of her own, she could be herself.

"One more dance, then."

"I . . . I've got to be going." She felt young, shy, inexperienced. "It must be getting very late."

"Not really. But whatever you say," Randy said after a pause. "I guess we can make out at your house as well as here. But we'd better tell Cass and Brew that I'll be back after awhile to take them to their car."

In the kitchen a half dozen boys and girls were eating pizza at the big round table in the breakfast room. Beer cans were piled on the counter and in the sink. There seemed to be a good deal of hilarity and Randy had to raise his voice before anyone heard his question. Had anyone seen Cass and Brew?

"Don't ask me," Biz Dudevant said, thickly. "Haven't seen 'em. Don't even know where Pris is. Prowling around somewhere, up to no good." A slight, dark-complexioned boy wearing black-framed glasses with heavy lenses, he looked, Robin thought, rather like a bad-tempered owl.

Someone else at the table laughed. "They might be downstairs. Somebody was down there playing Ping-pong a little while ago."

"They weren't down there five minutes ago when *I* came up," said another.

Randy shrugged. "It doesn't matter that much. They can't go without me. When you see Brew, tell him I'll be back after a while."

Robin shivered as they walked toward the car. But even after she was inside, with the heater on and Randy's arm around her as he drove, her feet felt like two chunks of ice. She could think of nothing to say at all as they approached the street where she lived.

Randy cut off the motor, doused the headlights, allow-ing the car to coast silently and in darkness until it came to a stop in front of Robin's house.

It really was an accident that they had kissed before, Robin thought, as Randy turned her face toward his. She'd not intended that first kiss at all.

Even so, all the authors of all the books on dating that she'd ever read, and all the writers of teen columns in magazines and newspapers, all of them—everyone—said that if you really liked a boy it was all right to give that boy a good-night kiss. But if you really didn't like him, and you still let him kiss you good night and in a very special way, and your conscience bothered you a bit, well then—what about that?

Robin turned her back on the small questioning voice. The solution to such a dreary problem was one that might as well be saved for later.

4

"I *did* tell the truth," Robin said to herself after she'd reported to her mother about the events of the evening before. "Maybe I just didn't tell *all* of it."

Actually, she had told very little of it at all. They had gone to Dinty's to get something to eat, she said, and there they had met a girl by the name of Pris Gosling who was buying pizzas and hamburgers and things for a little spur of the moment party she was giving. They'd stayed there until Randy brought her home.

"I assume Pris's parents were there," Mrs. James said, but that remark Robin pretended not to hear; she rushed on telling about all the new kids she'd met, and about all the different things there were to do at the Goslings. Dancing in the family room, Ping-pong in the basement, a five-thousand-piece jigsaw puzzle in the library (Cass had told her about that before they arrived) . . . *and necking everywhere*, her conscience added in a voice so loud that Robin could almost swear that her mother had heard it, too.

"We didn't get to see much of Randy," her mother said. "Or of Brew, either. You were all out the door before anyone could draw a deep breath."

"I know," Robin said apologetically. "It wasn't very nice. But it's a . . . kind of game."

"Not a very grown-up one, I'm afraid," her mother answered. Then suddenly she smiled. "But it's been a long time since I was young. I expect that I've forgotten some things that once seemed like fun."

Robin gave her mother a grateful smile. Boring in, keeping on saying something to make you feel bad like some mothers did, until you were about ready to scream or cry, was something her mother never did. It was Judy Hart's mother's worst fault—or so Judy said. Otherwise, she was just fine.

Judy, herself, did some boring in the following Wednesday evening when Robin went to the Harts', presumably to study. Until then they'd hardly had time to talk at all. Judy had known without having it spelled out to her, that a report on the evening could not take place over the telephone.

: 45 :

Robin's father dropped her off at Judy's on his way to the laboratory. He was so involved with grasshoppers that since Saturday night he had scarcely mentioned Randy at all. "I'll pick you up between ten thirty and eleven o'clock. No later. I promised your mother faithfully that tonight I'd get a good night's rest."

Robin smiled as she ran up the sidewalk. She loved to go to the Harts. There were so many of them, yet everything ran so smoothly. Not at all like the Digbys who lived down the street from the Jameses. Although they didn't have as many children as the Harts, the Digby kids' white shoes were always dirty.

Robin knocked. Someone yelled "Come in!" Robin did, speaking to the various Harts who came running. Judy, who was hanging over the upstairs bannister, hollered down above the tumult. "Bring your books and come on up. Don't let yourself get diverted."

It was a temptation not to. At least, for a little while. The only time she felt a trace of envy was at the Harts. That Judy should have such an array of brothers and sisters and that she should have none, did not seem quite fair. But as Judy said, that was a matter of viewpoint and the minute Robin was inside Judy's room a large hand-lettered KEEP OUT sign was put in place and the door firmly closed.

Robin threw her books on Judy's bed. "What shall we do first? Study and then talk or talk and then study?"

"Talk and then study," Judy said. "Now I promise not to say a word until you've told me everything that happened."

It was a promise that it was not possible to keep. Even so, Judy did quite well, contenting herself mostly with wise nods when Robin told about the mob they'd found hanging out at Dinty's and the necking that was going on in the big supermarket parking lot. But when it came to telling about Pris Gosling's party, Judy's expression became intense. "I've heard about those parties. But inviting Brew Winfield! That's the worst! That girl would do anything to get him away from Cass. I've seen her working on him at school, mooning around, looking at him with those big goo-goo eyes."

"I don't think Cass needs to worry," Robin said, not wishing to enlarge on her knowledge. "Brew likes her pretty well."

"I don't doubt that. It's just that Cass deserves somebody a darned sight nicer than that pill, if you ask me," Judy said, then her ominous tone brightened. "What I want to know, is how you got along with Pill Number Two?"

"I don't know whether to tell you or not—if you think he's such a pill."

"Why Robin James! How can you *not* tell me? Unless you've done something to be ashamed of."

"It's not that and you know it," Robin said, falling neatly into Judy's trap.

"Well, then you do like him. That's pretty plain to see."

Robin shook her head. With Judy's big myopic eyes upon her, she felt herself blushing. "I'm not even sure I like him at all. As a person, I mean."

"For Heaven's sake, how else could you like him—except as a person?"

"I don't know how to explain it," Robin said, and honestly she did not. "It . . . it's little things he does. The way he thinks . . . the way he feels about things . . ."

"Give me an example."

Judy had put on such a clinical expression as she scrootched forward to listen, that for a moment Robin debated telling her about Randy approving of Biz Dudevant's father talking to the judge and getting Biz out of his scrape with the law. But it didn't seem quite fair to hold it back. Judy, who was going to study human behavior and explore people's minds, ought to be the first to admit that Randy could not be held entirely at fault. How a person was raised and what influences he was exposed to could affect his whole life.

When Robin finished reporting the conversation the best she could remember, she looked up at Judy almost defiantly. "And I don't want you to think I'm defending Randy for thinking it's all right for Biz's father to do a think like that. It's just that I'm trying to understand him—to understand why he thinks a thing like that. I think he had a pretty crummy time growing up."

Judy gripped a handful of her hair with both fists. "Now what kind of logic is that? Lots of kids who have a crummy time growing up, turn out fine. And on the other hand you have somebody like Brew Winfield. His father's president of Winfield Manufacturing. His mother's 'old family.' He's had just about everything a kid could want—and look at him! He's as bad as Randy Griffin any day."

Robin gave a rueful little laugh. "I suppose. Actually, it doesn't make a lot of difference. Randy didn't like me well enough to ask me for another date. Just said 'See you' and went roaring off into the night."

"I wouldn't let that bother me," Judy said, practically.

"Still..."

The word had trailed off so wistfully that Judy looked up from the pile of books she had been pulling toward her across the desk.

"You really do like him, don't you?" There was faint wonderment in Judy's voice.

Robin considered a moment, then gave the most honest answer she could give. "Not with my head."

"Somebody's at the door for Robin." It was Jamie Hart, Judy's five-year-old sister. Dressed for bed and clutching an oversized Raggedy Ann, she stood outside the door when Judy opened it.

"Fathers!" Robin exclaimed exasperatedly. "He's not supposed to come and get me for hours."

"It's not your father," Jamie said, savoring the message to which she'd been intrusted. "It's a boy."

"A boy!" Robin felt she must be growing pale. She dispatched a grateful glance to Judy who had managed to thank Jamie profusely and still get the door shut again. Now she leaned with her back against it, as if it were in danger of being battered down.

Robin ran to the window. "It's Randy!" she gasped.

"What are you going to do?" Judy's practical nature was now coming to the fore. "You can't let him drive you home because your father is coming."

"I could call my father and tell him not to come." Now that Robin had spoken the words, the idea did not sound quite so preposterous. "After all, Randy wouldn't even know I'm here unless my mother told him. So it must be all right."

"I hope you know what you're doing," Judy said disapprovingly, "though I doubt it."

Robin was shaky as she went downstairs. The phone in the library, for once, was not in use. Also, fortunately, neither of Judy's parents were around as she dialed the number of her father's laboratory.

He was a long time answering but when he did and heard the purpose of Robin's call, he seemed relieved. "Good," he said. "And thank Mr. Hart for taking you home. In spite of what I told your mother, I'm afraid I'm going to be a good deal later finishing up here than I thought."

"It's O.K.," Robin said, as she turned away from the

phone. She hoped that Judy, whose ears were of the keenest had not overheard her father's end of the conversation. If her father had leaped to conclusions about who was taking her home, it was not her fault. "I'm sorry to be rushing off," she said, lamely, to Judy.

"Don't mind me, for Heaven's sake!" Judy put on her grand dame air. "You only come over to spend the evening with me and then off you go with a person who doesn't know any more than to wait for a girl outside in his car."

The words, however, were no sooner spoken than Judy asked to be forgiven. "I don't know what makes me so mean and hateful. Actually, you might be a most powerful influence for good in Randy's life. And anybody can change for the better. Look at St. Augustine. He was absolutely terrible. His mother had just about decided to give up on him when he decided to shape up."

Robin edged toward the door. Although she was glad Judy had had a change of heart about Randy driving her home, still when Judy really got warmed up on a subject she could go on for quite a while—though usually in a most interesting way.

"But on the other hand," Judy continued. "It might just work the other way around. Instead of you being an influence for good on *him*, he might be a bad influence on *you*."

"If I don't hurry up and get out there, nobody's going to be an influence on anybody."

She could hear Randy's car breathing heavily in the drive as she ran down the steps. The door swung open as she neared.

Then once again it happened and so easily it was frightening. She pushed herself from him. "No, Randy! Please. Not here!" Her breath came out in a little startled gasp.

Randy laughed softly. "We could have quite a thing going without any trouble at all."

"I don't know what you mean." She spoke stiffly, scrubbing her mouth with the back of her hand. "Now will you please start the car?"

"Sure thing," Randy said. "But I do think you know what I mean."

Robin stared straight ahead. Her cheeks were so hot she thought they must be glowing in the darkness. Angry at Randy and equally angry with herself she could not trust herself to speak.

Randy swerved the car, cutting in front of a small sports car that had passed him a few minutes before. He laughed softly, then relaxed his speed, half turning to face her. Both his smile and his voice were coaxing. "Don't be sore. I didn't mean to make you mad. But why kid ourselves? I like you. You like me. You can't help it any more than I can. What's the use of fighting it?" His arm which had been resting along the top of the seat slipped across her shoulders and quickly she pulled herself away.

What was it Cass had said in the car when they were

sitting in the parking lot at Dinty's eating hamburgers. "Don't mix her up, Randy. Don't try to double-talk her out of what she knows is right."

Randy was trying to do that now. His logic was wrong and his premise false—yet she hadn't the strength or the courage to refute it. "But as long as I'm not doing anything wrong," she said reassuringly to herself, "I needn't be ashamed."

She sat back in the half circle of Randy's arm as he made what he called "the rounds"—the hamburger hangouts, the "in" drugstores, the necking spots, and finally the downtown area where cars, three abreast, raced each other with tires squealing and brakes screeching around the dozen blocks that formed "the loop."

It was eleven o'clock by the dashboard clock as Randy stopped the car in the shadows a half block from her front door. "Better stop here," Randy said. "I don't want to make your mother any madder at me than she already is."

"What do you mean?" She spoke sharply in her alarm. "My mother knew that you were bringing me home."

"I'm afraid your mother doesn't know." There was an unpleasant undertone in Randy's voice. "In fact, after she said you were at Judy's studying, she told me rather pointedly it would not be necessary for me to bring you home. That you'd already made arrangements with your father."

"Why didn't you tell me? Why did you let me come?

You . . . you've ruined everything." In the darkness, Robin was reaching for her books that had gone skittering across the floor of the car.

"Listen, baby. Don't push the panic button." Randy's voice was cajoling. "Why shouldn't I bring you home? Why shouldn't you go out with anybody you want to? You're a big girl now. If I can't see you one way, I'll see you another."

Robin shook her head numbly. "I . . . I've got to go in. Right now."

"Five minutes can't make any difference," Randy said softly. "Just five minutes—to talk things over. O. K.?"

The door was unlocked, the porch light on. Robin let herself in.

Her father's hairy tweed topcoat was in the hall closet, his worn leather brief case lying on the table under the long mirror. She stared at herself, but it was a stranger who faced her, not the old Robin James at all.

Slowly, she climbed the stairs, stocking-footed— though it was too much to hope that her parents would be asleep. Passing their bedroom door her mother said "Good night, Robin" softly, and for a moment she stood there before she said "Good night" and went down the hall to her own room.

Guiltily, Robin sprang out of bed at the alarm clock's first ring. By hurrying she could be downstairs before her father left for the laboratory.

PART ONE: *Robin*

From the bottom step she could see both him and her mother standing in the front hall. The latter's head was slightly bent, one hand resting on her father's shoulder. They were talking in tones too low for her to hear.

"Daddy! Don't go for a minute." She came toward her parents with a little premeditated skip designed to express happiness and the confidence of full forgiveness. "I'm sorry about last night. Randy's sorry, too. But with Daddy working so late he thought it might be a help if he came to take me home."

"I'm glad if it was a misunderstanding," her father said. His voice was always gruff when he felt soft inside. Robin pressed the advantage.

"And he asked me out for Saturday night! We're doubling with Cass and Brew!" She gave her father a kiss on the little furrow between his brows and before anyone could say a word dashed back upstairs.

5

Not since she'd been in high school, could Robin remember making a worse mess of an exam. She looked down at the sheet of paper with its horrid blanks, vacant spaces, and erasures. French was not her best subject to begin with, and the new verbs—dreadful, irregular ones—that Mademoiselle Balthus had been throwing at them (as if she were determined to double the class's vocabulary in the five weeks that remained of school) had made no impression on her at all.

In other classes she had not fared much better during the past few weeks. Even in English, which she loved,

PART ONE: *Robin*

Miss Bird had sent back her outline for her junior theme with a red-penciled, "Not enough thought has gone into this."

With a wry little smile, Robin scribbled in what was sure to be a wrong answer. How could she give much thought to French verbs or to making an outline of *The Great Gatsby* when all she could think of was Randy Griffin? She hardly saw Judy Hart at all any more. Judy said she was "in the way." And in a way, she was. Randy was nice about driving her home, but he either did not care to draw her into the conversation or else lacked the social skill to do so. Judy just sat there lumpishly in the front seat beside them until Randy dropped her in front of her own house. And all the while Robin's heart was keeping time in some sort of a crazy offbeat fashion like, what was it—"The Love of Three Oranges"? Only this was the love of Randy Griffin. No, not *love*. Her mind rebelled at that. If you loved a boy you would be proud of him. She was not proud of Randy.

Nor was she happy. Certainly not at home. She could see and feel her mother and father watching her; sensed their pain and puzzlement. As little grains of silt and sand, each so tiny in themselves, build up until they divert a stream to a different course, so did each small lie or half truth make communication between them more difficult.

It had had its beginnings the night of her first date with Randy. Although she had not seen him a dozen times since then, after each meeting there was a little more to hold back or to explain away.

The bell rang. With a last forlorn glance Robin glanced down at the mishmash she'd made of the exam and added it to the pile of other papers being passed to the front of the room.

English, the last class of the day and her favorite, dragged on interminably. Would Randy be waiting for her today? The days he did not come she felt lost and almost ill. In her diary she had kept a record of their dates but even if she had not, each one was printed in her mind. The night he'd picked her up at Judy's house. The Saturday night they were supposed to be doubling with Cass and Brew and had never connected with them at all. One night the four of them had gone to a movie but it was only Randy's nearness that counted. The movie she could not remember at all. The other times he'd met her after school. Several times Cass and Brew had gone along and they'd driven to a nearby park. Cass and Brew had disappeared and though Randy had been his most disarming, she'd only let him kiss her. That was all.

The days Randy didn't come, his excuses were numerous. He was looking for a job and you had to take appointments when you could get them. His car developed a mysterious ailment. He'd tried, but failed, to reach her and say he couldn't come. Yet he always seemed so genuinely contrite that she forgave him. But not today. If he should come, she would make him take her straight home. Take Judy home, too. That would be punishment for not having picked her up the day before, or the day before that—though he'd called each night saying, "Sorry, baby. Tomorrow after school for sure."

She tried, unsuccessfully, to force a bright, alert expression as Miss Bird gave the assignment for the next day.

Class over, she waited outside the door for Judy who was forever coming out. In two more minutes she'd go on without her. She couldn't afford to wait longer for fear of missing Randy.

When Judy did come out, she shook her head at Robin's suggestion that she and Randy would drive her home. "I've some other things to do here at school first. You go on."

"Please?"

Again Judy shook her head, this time flushing so that her year-round freckles vanished in a sea of pink. "Can't you see that it's not any fun for me being with you and Randy? Can't you see I don't want you to feel sorry for me, or worry about me? Some place, somewhere there is a boy who is looking for me, and he'll know me when he finds me. And I'll know him. The perfect boy."

"Well, if that's the way you feel," Robin said a little stiffly. "I was only offering you a ride home."

"Thanks anyway," Judy said, a different friendly tone. "If you don't go out with Randy Saturday, maybe you could come over and spend the night."

"I . . . I'll have to see. I'll let you know."

Running in the corridors was prohibited but she did it anyway. When she reached her locker, she took out all her books. She would take them home. Every one. There was something in the way Judy had looked when she talked about "her boy" that had been like turning a sharp little screw of conscience deep inside her. If Randy asked her for a date for Saturday they would have a good talk first. They'd turn over a new leaf. Set the record straight.

If only he was waiting now.

He was.

"Mademoiselle," he said. He leaped out of the car, ran around to the other side and opened the door with a low bow. "Vool-aye-vooz."

He had mocked her like this since the day he'd picked up her French book and looked inside. "What do you want to study stuff like this for? Isn't English good enough for you?"

"Randy, don't!" she said now, so sharply that he cringed and put his arm up against his forehead as if he were fending off a mortal blow.

"I did terribly in the test." Even the sight of him could not counteract the memory of the paper she had handed in.

"Listen, baby." Randy was suddenly serious. "You got to correct your thinking. You feel bad now, sure. But what's it going to matter a hundred years from now? You're here. I'm here. The sun's shining. What's there to worry about?"

"Lots." She could not give up, or give in, easily. Randy was over-simplyfying. Still, there was something in what he said.

"Well, hop in," Randy said. "Let's be on our way. Fellow who lives out near Grimesville's got a car I want to look at. We can be out there and back in an hour and a half."

"I'll have to let my mother know." The words were spoken before Robin remembered her resolve to go straight home. But now it was too late to say anything about it. She could tell from Randy's expression that he was not pleased at the prospect of further delay. "It will just take a minute. There's one of those outdoor telephone booths on the corner across from the drug-store. I can call from there."

Fortunately, the booth was empty and Robin smiled encouragingly at Randy as she went inside and shut the folding door. Her mother answered almost at once and in one breathless sentence Robin spurted out her message. "I'm going to Grimesville with Randy to see this fellow. We'll be back by a little after five o'clock. O.K.?"

Waiting for her mother's familiar, "All right, dear. Be careful," Robin felt a twinge of impatience. It really should not take her mother so long to reply. Or nuisance of nuisances, the connection might be broken. "Mama, are you there?"

"Yes, dear, I'm here," her mother said. "I was thinking. Thinking that you'd best come on home."

"Mother, please!" Robin spoke softly, imploringly. From the booth she could see Randy glancing at his watch and pulling down his mouth in a way that made him not look handsome at all. "Maybe we won't even be gone that long. It's so pretty and springy out. And we'll be careful. Mother, I promise."

"No, Robin. We'll talk about it later."

Slowly, Robin put down the phone. Her mother's voice had been pleasant, firm, and final.

"I'm sorry, Robin." Mrs. James had knocked before entering.

Although Robin still stood staring out the window she could see her mother as clearly as if she faced her.

"I think it would be easier to talk to you, dear, if you'd turn around."

Robin turned, scuffing the toe of her shoe back and forth against the leg of her desk chair. She knew the gesture was childish, she felt a twinge of shame, but still she did not speak.

"I think you know that neither your father nor I approve of your . . . friendship with Randy. The sooner it is ended, the easier it will be. That's why I asked you to come home this afternoon."

"You wouldn't!" Robin cried out sharply, startled from her pose. "You can't make me not see him any more!"

"Your father and I don't want to make you do any-thing. We think that in your heart you know Randy isn't your kind of boy."

"But what if I *don't* decide that? What if I do go on seeing him in spite of you and Daddy? What if I told you . . ." Robin's quivering angry voice faded to silence. Even to punish her mother she could not say, "What if I told you I love him." She threw herself face down on the bed and did not move until her mother left the room.

Nor did Robin go down to dinner. Instead, she en-dured grumbly hunger pangs all evening as she sat at her desk trying to put some "thought" into her outline on *The Great Gatsby*.

Several times she cautiously opened her bedroom door and hung over the upstairs bannister listening to the low murmur of her parents' voices. Although she could only catch a word here and there it was enough to know that they were not talking about her. It did not make her completely glad.

The evening dragged on, the telephone not ringing even once. Since she'd been dating Randy, Judy seldom called. And it was unlikely that she'd hear from Randy. His mood had not been of the best when he'd dropped her in front of her house that afternoon. Shivering with uneasiness, Robin dug out a pair of flannel pajamas that she'd discarded only a week before in favor of a summer nightie and turned down the covers on her bed.

In the darkness, tears seeped from her tightly closed

eyes and made sad damp places on her pillow. "To-morrow, and to-morrow, and to-morrow . . . creeps in this petty pace from day to day . . ." She'd liked those lines and memorized them earlier in the year when they'd studied *Macbeth*. They would have new meaning if she did not see Randy again. *If* she did not see him again . . .

A little later when a tap came at her door and her father softly called her name, she made her heart hard to him and did not answer.

Although it meant telling Judy everything, still without her a plan could not have been worked out. It was she who thought of writing him a note. Not only would it be more difficult to tell Randy in person, she insisted, but it would be embarrassing for both of them. No, a note was the proper way to handle the situation. And she would deliver it to him in person.

Before Robin copied it in its final form, the girls read it over together:

"Dear Randy: My mother and father think it would be a good idea if we did not see each other for a while. I hope that before too long they will change their minds. Love, Robin."

Judy had wanted Robin to sign the letter "Your friend," but Robin had held out for "love." "It's just a word," Robin said. "I don't mean it in the sense of really *love*, but I think it will kind of soften the blow."

"I think you've softened it enough already," Judy replied with some asperity, "by saying that your parents don't want you to see Randy 'for a while,' when they really mean that they don't want you *ever* to see him again."

"But what if they change their minds!" Robin cried. "They might, you know, if I should begin to pine away."

"That," Judy said, with an unromantic snort, "I'd like to see."

But maybe I'll change my mind.

Three days had passed since Judy, waiting outside school for Randy, had handed him the note. Since then, the thought had passed through Robin's head a hundred times. Even if her parents did disapprove, what would be the harm in seeing Randy now and then after school? What would be wrong in meeting him at the Public Library? Or at somebody's house for a party? Could there be anything so sinful in that? She wouldn't feel so bad if Randy hadn't taken the news so hard.

Even Judy had looked quite bleached out and pale as she reported back to Robin who'd been nervously waiting in the school library. "He took it, said 'What's this' and when I said it was a note from you, he got an ugly expression on his face and said I don't read 'Dear John' letters, baby. Tell your little friend *I* know why she's chicken, and I think she knows it, too.' Then he ripped

: 65 :

the envelope this way and that in about a jillion pieces and roared away in his car."

Robin had not seen him since.

Downstairs, the telephone rang. She pushed back her desk chair and ran for the stairs but stopped mid-point as her mother's voice came up to her.

"If Will isn't too tired, we'd love to. Just a minute and I'll ask him." There was a little silence then a cheery, "Will says 'yes.' We'll see you in just a little while."

Almost before Robin could get back to her room her mother was ascending. "That was the Brookes. They've just got back the colored slides they took in Trinidad and want to show them to Daddy and me. I should say 'me' because I'm afraid they will be pretty 'birdy' but your father insists he's wild to see them, too. We shouldn't be too late. But on the other hand, there might be a lot of pictures, too."

"That's all right," Robin mumbled. "I've got plenty of studying to do." Her tone was ungracious and she knew it. She had read a thousand times that if a person wanted to be treated as an adult, she was supposed to learn to act like an adult. She did not care. She wanted to act childish.

Her mother said "Good-bye" and again Robin mumbled a reply. Owlishly she stared down at the mass of undone homework before her. The house was very still. Carrie Chapman came upstairs on her foggy cat feet, looked around, uttered a single, mournful mew and disappeared as silently as she had come.

In this silence, the ringing of the telephone sounded as shatteringly loud as a fire siren. Robin ran to answer it, deciding on the way it would be her mother or father calling to be sure the electric coffee pot was unplugged or the front door securely latched.

Already a bit ashamed of the way she'd acted, Robin adopted a falsely cheery voice when she said "Hello."

There was no answer from the other end of the line, only a soft breathing silence.

"Hello!" she said again, but this time uneasily. There was someone there. Before he said a word she knew it was Randy.

"Saw your folks drive away," he said. "Be right over."

The telephone grew slippery in her nervous fingers as she tried to frame a reply. She held it away from both ear and mouth as if fearful the sudden thumping of her heart might communicate a message of its own. But before she could frame a single word, she heard the full, final emptiness that follows the click of the receiver.

He was coming. He was coming without even waiting for her reply. And he could not be far away. Less than ten minutes had passed since her parents had left the house.

She ran almost blindly to the front door not knowing whether to check the lock or fling wide the door. Already she could hear the throbbing of the car's motor as it came to a stop in front of the house. Its headlights were blacked out.

The heavy, brassy sound of the front knocker was

drowned in the heavy, muffled beating of her own heart.

Robin's hand moved in slow motion toward the door knob. No one would know if she let Randy come in. The Hawthornes, their closest neighbors, were out of town. Old Mrs. Bassett who lived on the other side never unglued herself from her television set long enough to know what was going on in the real-life world.

Something stayed her hand. "Never unlock the door to anyone, ever, unless you first look to see who's there. That's why Daddy had the architect design this little look-through when he built the house." Her mother's words, so often repeated that they were as familiar to her as her own name, played themselves like a reflex in her head.

Robin, on her side of the door, turned the little brass knob that allowed the small diamond-shaped window within the door to open. Through the now exposed grill, she could see the two dark mocking eyes, the flash of white teeth, the crooked smile. It was Randy, all right.

"O.K., O.K. Enough fun and games," Randy said. "Let me in."

Robin's hand did not move. Nor did it seem to belong to her at all.

"Listen, baby. Quit clowning. Let's give the thing we've got going a chance. Why else do you think I've been hanging around your house for the last three nights, waiting for a chance to see you alone. All alone."

PART ONE: *Robin*

For a moment Robin felt, dizzy, confused, a little ill. Like a fast-moving, speeded-up film, its details obscured, her life as yet unlived unrolled before her. She could make of it anything she wished. Somewhere out there, and sometime—for her as for Judy—the perfect boy would come along. He would know her when he found her—and she would know him. Although at this distance she could not hope to see his face, one thing was clear. It wasn't Randy.

Once again her heart began beating in a most comfortable and normal way. "Sorry, Randy," she said softly. "Not tonight. Not ever." With a firm hand she closed the little brass door.

She was in her room studying an hour later when her parents came home.

Her mother looked in. "Anyone call while we were gone?"

"Someone did call," said Robin, " . . . but it was a wrong number."

PART TWO

Cass

I

If Robin had not stopped by her locker after lunch period she would not have found the note when she did. Then, stooping over to pick up a book that had fallen, she saw the piece of paper folded envelope-shape that had been slipped through a crack near the floor.

Without taking time to read it through, she glanced at the blocky signature and sighed. Cass. Several times before Cass had left notes for her like this. But always before they'd had something to do with plans Brew and Randy had made. But now that was all over and done. Like a person who steps outdoors for the first time after recovering from a long illness, she felt clean and renewed. Nothing Cass could do or say or write in any note would ever make her see Randy again.

Even so, as she read the note she felt a stirring of resentment. "Meet me at the door of the cafeteria just before first lunch period," Cass had scribbled. "I *have* to see you."

Robin crumpled the note and stuffed it in the pocket of her dress, her resentment subsiding with the act. She didn't blame Cass. Cass was a tool. Cass did whatever Brew wanted her to do. Why Brew made Cass do what Randy wanted, however, was anybody's guess.

Judy Hart had one. "Randy's got something on him, I bet. Sort of a friendly blackmail. You know the police never did find out who tied that Greeley High gym suit to the top of the TV tower. It could have been Brew."

It could have, indeed. More than once Robin had heard the two boys make allusions to one escapade or another. But that, too, all belonged to the past. All that remained of that chapter was Cass. And Cass—warm, accepting, and generous—was still her friend.

Robin glanced at the big wall clock overhead. Five minutes remained before her next class. Although she had missed meeting Cass at the time and place she had specified, she might still find her and tell her that Randy was out of her system for good.

Before Robin reached Cass's locker the crowds in the corridors had thinned out to such a degree that she could see that Cass was not there. A ninth-grader, a girl Robin knew slightly, was fumbling with the key to a nearby locker. She looked up.

"Cass Carter's been looking for you. She said for me to tell you if I saw you." She nodded her head in the direction of the girls' toilet. "She went in there."

The L-shaped room was large, windowless, brightly lighted and permeated with the faint, sickly sweet odor of disinfectant. A long bank of lavatories ran along two walls. A mirror the length of each bank was above them. Cass was not in sight.

Robin called Cass's name softly. Then again, louder. "Cass!"

Almost at the same moment Cass appeared. Her cheeks were tear-stained and her eyes red-rimmed.

Robin rushed forward. "What's wrong? What happened? Are you sick?" Without waiting for a reply, she dug in her shoulder bag for a handkerchief and thrust it toward Cass who was dabbing at her eyes with a small damp wad of tissue.

The sigh Cass gave in response was so long, indrawn, and quavering that Robin felt tears springing to her own eyes.

"Do you hurt somewhere? If it's in your side maybe it's your appendix. Before I had mine out, I thought I was going to die. Do you want me to take you to the nurse so you can lie down for a little while?"

"No! Not the nurse!" Although Cass cried out in alarm, the suggestion seemed to help compose her.

"When you didn't meet me at the cafeteria before lunch and I couldn't find you afterward, I came down here to ... to put on some lipstick, and then I ... I don't know ... I just began to cry."

"That's nothing to cry about," Robin said practically. "I didn't meet you for the simple reason I didn't find your note until a few minutes ago. But now you'd better hurry up and tell me what's the matter. The first bell has already rung."

Cass walked over to the mirror as if her legs were made of sticks. Though seeming to look at herself, she was really looking with expressionless eyes at Robin whose face was also reflected in the mirror.

"I . . . I wanted to ask you about a doctor. Your father's a doctor. He . . . he seemed so nice. Maybe I could go to him. But not about my appendix. It's . . . it's more about my stomach."

Robin laughed a little nervously. "My dad's nice, but he's not that kind of a doctor. He's a Ph.D—Doctor of Philosophy. A scientist. Your parents must have a doctor, though. Couldn't you go to him?"

Cass turned, shook her head almost fiercely. "No, I can't. Don't you know anything? If . . . if there's this certain something wrong with me and my dad found out, he'd kill me."

"Oh." Robin's voice was bleak. She began to feel quite sick inside herself. "It couldn't be *that*. You and Brew haven't ... you couldn't ..."

Cass's wide-eyed terrified nod was answer enough. "I'm afraid to find out. I'm afraid not to. In the morning my stomach feels so funny I can't eat. My mother looks at me so queerly. Sometimes I think I want to die . . ."

"Don't talk like that! Don't ever say such a thing. Maybe that's not what is wrong with you at all. Once, I missed a period."

"I . . . I missed two. The second one has just gone by." Cass whispered the words.

Robin could not help staring as comprehension became complete. "But Brew . . . What does he think? What does he say? What are you going to do?"

"I haven't told him. This last week I haven't even seen him much. There's a golf tournament he's playing in, and his grades . . . if he doesn't bring his grade in English up he's not going to graduate."

The door from the corridor opened, then swung shut with a swish. It was followed by a light tinkling laugh.

"What goes on here," Pris Gosling asked, "that you two children are not in class?" She looked at Cass with wide-set pale blue eyes. "And tears, too. Dear, dear." With an obvious flourish she placed her "pink slip," the tangible evidence that she was out of class legitimately, on the lavatory counter while she deliberately removed her old lipstick and made a new mouth.

The silence was so awkward that Robin could not help but fill it. "Cass doesn't feel well."

Pris moistened a forefinger with her tongue, smoothed

her eyebrows and smiled at her reflection. "Tough luck."

"But I feel better now." Cass spoke with a brightness Robin would have thought impossible before Pris had entered. The minute Pris had sailed out, however, Cass began to whimper. "I don't feel so awfully good right this minute."

Cass didn't look so awfully good, either, Robin thought. There was a white rim around her mouth and her forehead was misted with dampness.

"Maybe you've got a virus. You could have. Or it might be something you ate. But anyway, a doctor will know. I'll help you find one. Someone nice."

"I . . . I'm afraid to go alone."

"I'll go with you if you want me to," Robin said soothingly. "Now, maybe if you went up to the nurse's office and lay down for a little while you'd feel better."

Cass shook her head. "I'll be all right. I really will. But you'd better not wait for me any longer. You'll have to go to Mrs. Dempsey to get back in class as it is."

"I know. But I'll just tell her the truth. That you got sick and I just stayed with you for a little while."

"No, not that!" Cass clutched imploringly at Robin's hand. "I don't want her to know I'm sick. She mustn't know anything about it."

"Well, then, I'll just tell her that some girl—a girl I didn't know—got sick and that I stayed with her for a little while. You're really sure you feel all right?"

Cass nodded, giving Robin a weak grateful smile. But

PART TWO: *Cass*

not until she took a comb from her purse and began to
do something to her hair did Robin decide that it was
safe to leave. Feeling a little ill herself she walked down
the long corridor, her footsteps echoing strangely in its
between-class emptiness, to the office of the Girls' Advisor. The door was shut. One girl was waiting ahead of
her. She looked up when Robin came in.

"Be my guest. Take a chair," she said, shifting a wad
of gum to the other side of her mouth. "What are you in
for?"

"Just a pink slip to get back into class." Robin's mouth
was dry.

"Me, too," the girl with the gum said. "Thank God!
Whoever's in there now," she jerked her head toward
the closed door, "musta killed somebody."

Robin, sitting nervously on the edge of the yellow-
varnished chair, watched as the other took out a long
steel nail file and with rhythmic, rapier-like movements
proceded to sharpen the points on her already pointy
nails.

Watching her was better than thinking. Anything was
better than that. If she even let her mind dwell for a
moment on the conversation she had had with Cass, she
began to panic. Something would have to be done. A
doctor would have to be found. An appointment made.
You just couldn't go walking in . . .

The door to the office opened and a girl sauntered out.
Whatever she had done, she did not look repentant.

The girl with the gum went in, was out a few minutes

later, pink slip in hand. She seemed to have swallowed her gum. She winked. "Next case."

"All right, Robin. What brings you here?" Mrs. Dempsey said. She smiled, but it was a tired smile. When she took off her glasses and lay them on her desk to rub her temples briefly, Robin noticed her eyes. They were blue, black-lashed and really quite beautiful. But with her glasses back on she was Mrs. Dempsey again.

Robin swallowed. "I was in the rest room right after my lunch period and some girl got sick. I stayed with her until she was feeling better." It was the truth, every word the truth, yet the words came out as if she were speaking with a mouthful of cotton.

Mrs. Dempsey looked up from the little pad of pink slips that she now drew toward her. "Who was the girl, Robin?"

"I . . . I don't know. Just a girl."

There was a little pause before Mrs. Dempsey said, "I see," and wrote Robin's name above her stamp-pad signature.

2

Physicians and Surgeons. Robin had no idea there
were so many. And of so many varieties. Allergy and
Anesthesiologist, Gastro-Intestinal, Genito-Urinary, and
Gynecology. Just reading the names made Robin feel as
if she had a fever.

If only she had not offered to find a doctor for Cass, if
only she had not agreed to go along, Cass might have
gone to their own family doctor, Dr. Schaeffer. But that
was too risky. Not for Cass but for her! If Dr. Schaeffer
should come popping out of his office and into the waiting room and saw her sitting there, he might mention it

to her parents. Then there would be questions she did not know how to answer.

Robin's finger wavered a little as it ran up and down the columns in the yellow pages of the telephone book. There was a certain kind of doctor who made a speciality of the kind of thing that Cass might have wrong with her. She thought she might recognize the word if she saw it.

There it was. Obstetrics. Of the thirty or more names listed, she recognized only one. He officed in the same clinic as Dr. Schaeffer so that eliminated him.

Robin sighed. If only she could talk to Judy! Judy could tell her the name of the doctor who brought all her brothers and sisters. She would also be full of the most excellent advice on how to proceed with the matter at hand. Of course, she had not promised not to tell but so far a sense of delicacy restrained her. However, if she did not mention Cass by name . . .

Almost automatically, Robin's fingers found the proper little holes on the dial of the telephone. Although she was alone in the house, her voice dropped to a whisper when Judy answered.

"Could you come over for a little while? I've something terribly important to ask you."

"Can't. You come here," Judy said succinctly. "Mom's gone and I'm baby-sitting."

"My mother's gone with the car, but I can ride my bike. That'll save time. But we'll have to be alone."

"Don't worry about that. I have my ways."

PART TWO: *Cass*

Judy did. Although rumblings, thumpings, squeals, and the sound of running feet were heard from time to time as the various Harts disported themselves about the house, the girls were left undisturbed.

Robin told her story. Cass, of course, remaining anonymous—just a girl Robin had found crying in the rest room. And for once, Judy didn't say a word until after Robin, her voice a little shaky, had concluded.

"A baby! Oh, no!" Judy spoke thickly from behind the hand that she had clapped over her mouth. "Has she told her parents?"

Robin shook her head. "No. Nobody. Not even—the boy. First, she wants to find out for sure. You know, to find out if it's a baby that's making her sick. That's why she's got to go to a doctor. I thought maybe the one your mother goes to for babies. I couldn't remember his name."

"Dr. Munzinger," Judy said promptly. "Dr. Something Munzinger. Mother likes him, but I don't know about Cass."

Robin felt as if all her blood were draining away. "I . . . I didn't say it was Cass."

"I know you didn't. But who else could it be? No girl is going to come up to some perfect stranger she meets in the toilet and say 'Help me find a doctor because I think I'm going to have a baby.'"

All the while Judy was talking, Robin kept shaking her head and saying, "No!" as emphatically as she could, but Judy paid no attention. Her mind, Robin could see, was already wrestling with the problem.

"You might as well call while you're here," Judy said at last. "You can't very well be making an appointment with an obstetrician with your mother and father listening."

"I guess that's right," Robin said bleakly. "I just wish I hadn't said I'd do it."

"But you did," Judy said, now brisk. She thrust the phone toward Robin. "The number is . . ." She paused, her finger holding the place in the phone book. "First, you're going to have to say who the appointment is for."

"Can't I say Cass Carter?"

"Use your head, Robin. You're not thinking." Judy's tone was as patient and long suffering as a mother trying to get something through the head of a backward child.

"Oh. I guess not." Robin was meek.

"Of course, the name she *ought* to use," Judy added severely, "is Mrs. Brewster Bailey Winfield, the Third. But I guess she can't do that until they're married."

"Maybe she could call herself plain Mrs. Bailey."

"Mrs. Bailey." Judy repeated the name judicially, then added, "Mrs. Winfield Bailey. That will do nicely. Now all you have to do is call for an appointment."

"I can't!" Robin cried. She drew her hand back from the telephone. "I can't make myself say the words. It's too awful. You do it."

Judy, who it seemed had been making it almost a game, suddenly looked peakedy. "I guess I can't, either.

It . . . it's different when you think of it happening to you."

Two days passed before Robin summoned the courage to make the call. Then pity for Cass won out.

"I'd like to make an appointment for Mrs. Winfield Bailey," she told the slick, brisk voice that answered the telephone. "On Saturday, please."

"Dr. Munzinger can see you at one thirty Saturday afternoon. Will you repeat your name and give me your address, please?"

The name slipped glibly enough from Robin's tongue, but when it came to making up an address all thought left her.

"Are you there?" The voice was impatient.

If it had not been for the small calendar on the desk before her, she would have been lost. "Nineteen sixty-six May Street." She spoke the words feebly then hung up the receiver just as her mother's car turned in the driveway.

Although there had been no problem when Robin told her mother she wanted to go down town and look for summer clothes—she'd had a clothing allowance since the first of the year and consequently did a lot more looking before she bought—the problem had come in getting out of the house.

When her mother asked if she was meeting Judy and she said "No," her mother had assumed that she was not meeting anybody. "In that case," her mother said, "there's no hurry. You can clean up your room before you go."

She wiggled her way out of that and managed to arrive breathlessly at one twenty, the time she and Cass had agreed on, at the corner of Hampstead and Vine. There was no busier intersection in the city and no more favored place to meet than the spot where she stood, under the big bank's revolving clock. It was a location handy to everything, including the Woodbine building where Dr. Munzinger had his office.

By stepping back a foot or two, Robin could see the face of the clock whose big hand now clicked downward toward one twenty-five. She looked in all four directions but nowhere among the hurrying pedestrians could she see the flash of Cass's bright hair.

Of course, she might not come at all. The thought was not new to Robin's mind. The very day after Robin called and made the appointment with the doctor, Cass had been feeling better. Perhaps it was just nerves after all.

A second, later, Robin saw her. She was wearing a Kelly green shift that she'd made herself and with her bright hair and the pallor that changed her creamy complexion to milky white, Robin thought she looked beautiful.

Robin managed the most cheerful smile she could. "Come on, Mrs. Bailey. We're going to have to hurry like everything." As she spoke, she looked down at the pale, long-fingered hand that Cass had placed on her arm as they met. "Oh, my goodness! I just thought of something! If you're going to be Mrs. Bailey, you're going to have to have a ring . . ." She paused, hating to say it. " . . . A wedding ring."

Cass stared down at her hand as if she had never seen it before, then thrust it behind her as a frightened child might do.

"There's a dime store two doors down. It's on our way to the doctor's office. Come on." Cass came along, walking like one half awake, stopping when Robin did in front of the jewelry counter.

"We want a wedding ring," Robin told the girl who languidly came toward them. Robin had blurted out the words, not thinking how they sounded.

The clerk winked a heavily made-up eye. "We get a lot of cheapskate guys coming in here to buy a wedding ring for some sucker of a girl, but not too many girls come in to buy them for themselves."

"My friend happens to be buying it for a play we are going to give at school." Robin's tone was so cold that she, herself, shivered as the words came out. "She plays the role of a married woman." Ever after she was to wonder at her inventiveness. At once, the clerk's manner changed.

"Par'n me. No offense intended. The wedding rings are here in this section."

Robin stared at them. Symbols. She'd never really thought about it before—what a wedding ring really meant.

She gave her head a little shake as she remembered the role *she* was playing. "Those ninety-eight cent ones look good enough for a play," she said, her tone still chilly, and to Cass, "If that one you've got on fits all right, we'll take it. Here, I'll pay."

"Two cents tax makes it a dollar even," the clerk said, ingratiatingly. "Want me to put it in a sack?"

"Please," Robin said. "But we're in a hurry."

In the lobby of the Woodbine building, Cass put on the ring. Looking down at her hand tears began to leak from her eyes.

"You cry and I'm going straight home," Robin hissed. She did not care who heard her.

"I . . . I'm not crying."

"Well, all right then. There's an elevator going up. Come on."

Pressed back against the wall by a crush of passengers there was no opportunity to talk as the elevator shot upward. When they got off they were followed by a large motherly-looking woman. With her was a small boy who, on the elevator, had been concealed by a forest of legs.

When the girls paused to let the woman and little boy get ahead of them, she paused, too. "You girls look a little lost. If you'll just tell me where you're headed, perhaps I can help you. There are a lot of offices on this floor and if you make the wrong turn you can wander around for a week."

"Dr. Munzinger." Robin's voice was so quavery that she feared she could not answer at all.

"Oh!" said the woman. She could not keep her eyes from making a hurried appraisal of them both. "This *is* a coincidence. Dr. Munzinger is in the same office as the doctor I go to. If I don't miss my guess, and I don't think I do, number four is on the way. You girls just follow me."

Fortunately, the empty chairs in the reception room were arranged in such a way that the girls were separated from the woman of the elevator. Even more fortunately, they had not waited more than a painful ten minutes when a nurse appeared in a doorway across the room. "Mrs. Bailey. Mrs. Bailey, please."

Cass looked numb.

"That's you." Robin accompanied the whispered words with a sidewise kick at Cass who, before identifying herself to the receptionist, had sat opening and shutting the clasp on her purse until Robin had made her stop.

"Oh," Cass mumbled. "I . . . I guess I wasn't listening."

Robin stared at her lap, counting slowly to twenty-five, then to fifty, before she raised her eyes. Cass was gone. Even then she felt the pressure of unshed tears behind her burning lids. Coming to see Dr. Munzinger should be a happy thing for a person to do. One shouldn't come sneaking in with lies and a dime store wedding ring and tears.

The unpleasant train of thought was interrupted as someone sat down in the chair Cass had vacated.

"I know it isn't any of my business," said the woman of the elevator, "but just how old is your little friend?" Although she spoke in a whisper, it was loud enough for everyone in the room to hear.

"Eighteen." Robin's voice trembled over the lie. Cass's seventeenth birthday was barely past.

"I wouldn't have guessed her that old." The woman gave Robin a close appraising look. "And you're no more than sixteen." She sniffed. "Well, all I can say is that I hope she's married."

"Oh! yes! She's married!" Robin's voice rang out falsely and too loud. She looked up in panic. Every pair of eyes in the room was staring at her.

Robin picked up a magazine from a table beside her and tried to read. The words ran tearily together on the page. Not because of the woman or of what she'd said, but because of Cass. What was happening in there behind closed doors? Cass would have to answer questions, take off her clothes and be examined. "Dear God," she prayed, "please let it be nerves and not a baby."

If it was a baby, what would Cass do? She'd said her father would kill her. Of course, he would not. But Robin shivered remembering the one time she'd seen him.

If it *was* a baby, first of all Cass would have to tell Brew. During the past week when Cass had been feeling so bad she'd hardly seen him.

PART TWO: *Cass*

Robin put her hand up to her burning cheek. She would not think about Cass and Brew getting married. Not yet. Not till she knew. Cass won't have to tell me, Robin thought. The minute she comes through that door, I'll know. Robin looked at her watch. Forty-five minutes had crawled by. It couldn't be much longer. Nor was it.

Robin felt a chill pass the length of her spine. Cass came through the door walking as if she were blind, one hand held before her feeling the darkness. A nurse was a step behind her. "You're sure you're all right . . . Mrs. Bailey? You could lie down in doctor's office until you felt better."

Robin stood up. She doesn't see me, Robin thought. "Here I am, Cass. This way. Here's the door." She did not care who was looking, care what they thought or were whispering to each other behind their hands. She picked up Cass's purse which she'd left in her chair, leaped forward, opened the door, and herded Cass through.

"Can you walk? Do you think you're going to faint? We can get a cab. I've plenty of money, I think, to take you home."

Cass shook her head, woodenly allowed Robin to lead her toward the elevator. There she leaned back against the wall as if it alone were holding her up, looked at Robin and in a high, clear, quite expressionless voice said, "In seven months I'm going to have a baby. I've a prescription to get filled that will help my morning sickness.

I have a prescription for iron pills to build up my blood and calcium pills for my teeth. I have a prescription for everything—except a father for my baby . . ."

"You've got Brew . . ." Cass looked so strange Robin scarcely said the words aloud.

"Oh, yes, Brew," Cass said. Neither her voice nor her face changed expression. "I'll have to tell him. And I'll have to tell my parents."

"But not until you've told Brew," Robin said in alarm. "Not until . . . until you've got things settled."

"But that might be a little while. He's playing golf in that state tournament today. Tomorrow there's something doing, too."

"I'd still wait," Robin said, stubbornly.

"Do you think I wouldn't if I could!" Cass cried. Anger seemed to give her life. "I haven't any choice. If I don't tell my parents right away, the doctor says *he* will. That's because he thinks I need support. Support!" She laughed harshly. "If he only knew my dad . . ."

"But you said you were Mrs. Bailey . . ." Robin spoke falteringly. " . . . You're wearing a wedding ring."

"The ring didn't fool him for a minute. As soon as I started crying, he knew."

The elevator came and the girls were silent as it bore them downward. On the street, Cass took the ring from her finger and tossed it in the gutter. For a while the small imitation gold hoop rolled gaily along, then disappeared between the iron grids of a grating in the street.

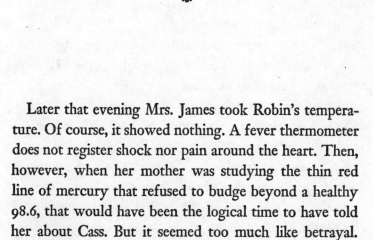

3

Later that evening Mrs. James took Robin's temperature. Of course, it showed nothing. A fever thermometer does not register shock nor pain around the heart. Then, however, when her mother was studying the thin red line of mercury that refused to budge beyond a healthy 98.6, that would have been the logical time to have told her about Cass. But it seemed too much like betrayal. She could not bring herself to do it.

At bedtime, her mother prescribed an aspirin and a glass of warm milk. On general principles, she said. This helped not at all, however, to dispel the sad little scenes that kept projecting themselves over and over in Robin's mind. The way Cass had looked as she came out of the doctor's office. Cass speaking in that high, clear unnatural voice. "In seven months I'm going to have a baby." Cass's face as she had thrown the wedding ring that was not a wedding ring at all, into the gutter. The sad stoop of Cass's shoulders as she got on the bus that would take her home.

What had happened since then, Robin could not envisage. It was too painful to try. Yet all night long she slept fitfully. Once, she dreamed she could see Cass cringing in front of her father, her arms raised in supplication, weeping soundlessly. She awoke. Before she slept again it was almost morning.

When her mother cautiously opened the door and looked in, Robin stirred and opened her eyes. To her surprise, her bedside clock said ten o'clock.

Her mother was carrying a big glass of orange juice. "Freshly squoze," she said, smiling. "And when you're ready, I'll bring you some breakfast."

Robin let the first delicious swallow of the orange juice trickle down her throat before she said a word. "Lovely. But I'm not sick. Really." With the sun streaming in, the pleasant sound of church bells ringing in the distance, she did indeed feel better. And too much dooming and glooming around might bring questions about the trip downtown the day before; questions that Robin, a poor liar, would be at a loss to answer.

"Oh, let me spoil you." A nostalgic smile crossed her mother's face. "Do you remember when you were little how much you liked to be sick? Not really sick, but just sick enough to have to stay in bed?"

Robin nodded. For a moment she was back in that happy time of childhood. A "sick-box" for each day in bed—a box filled with the most wondrous things: spools, gay colored threads, and beads. Buttons, bows, bits of lace and velvet, a baby doll to dress. . . . Tears stung her eyes and she looked away.

"One breakfast coming right up," her mother said briskly.

Robin barely had time to wash her face and brush her teeth before her mother was back with a tray. It held a tiny pitcher with a dozen violets, a big mug of cocoa with a marshmallow melting on top, a buttery stack of cinnamon toast.

The Sunday paper, in a not-too-tidy bundle was tucked under her mother's arm. "When your father gets through with the paper it looks as if it had been read by a dozen people. I haven't had a chance to look at it myself, but he says there's a picture of Cass's friend, Brew, in the sports section. About golf, or something." About anything that dealt with sports, Mrs. James was vague. She let the paper drop to the bed and placed the tray on Robin's lap. "Daddy and I are off to church, but there's no need for you to get up until you feel like it. Once during the night I heard you making such a strange noise

I got up to see what was the matter. But you were sleeping. Bad dreams?"

Robin nodded. If her mother pursued the matter, she could say she did not remember what she had dreamed about. But there was no need to fabricate. Her mother leaned over, brushed a kiss across her forehead, and left the room.

Not until Robin heard the car leave the drive did she look for the sports section. Only during the football season did she read this part of the paper at all. Then, when one was screaming one's self hoarse at the games, watching every move of every man on the field, it was fun to read about what you had seen and to see it again through the eyes of the reporters and photographers.

A black streamer of type ran across the top of the page.

WINFIELD WINS CITY GOLF MEET.

There, grinning up at her, cocky, confident, and happy was Brew, "Full of himself." It was an expression of her mother's, one that had come down to her from an Irish grandmother, and it fit Brew perfectly. A story about the meet ran down the right-hand side of the page, Robin did not read it all. Brew had won by the narrowest of margins. Bad luck had dogged his opponent, Marv Trotter of George Washington High, all through the meet. Brew had been lucky.

A crowd from both schools had followed the players around. There was a picture of the crowd, too, on an inside page. Among the spectators, and clearly recognizable in the front row, was Randy. Robin had not seen him since he appeared at her front door the night her parents were away.

She took the paper, crumpled it, and pushed it as far down in her wastebasket as it would go. Randy's face still was printed on the retina of her eye. Thinking about him still hurt. Judy said that in time this feeling would go away. Though how Judy knew, Robin could not imagine. "You're still a little schizoid over him, but that's only natural. It's like my dad quitting smoking. He says he really doesn't want to smoke any more because he knows it's bad for him, but that as long as he lives he'll remember how much he enjoyed it at the time."

Whether Judy's comparison was sound or not, Robin did not know but all thought of Randy vanished as she had a second thought about the picture so precipitously stuffed in the wastebasket. In the picture, a girl had been standing on either side of Randy. Thinking only of Randy at that moment, she had not given the girls a second glance. She retrieved the paper, smoothed it out on the floor the best she could. One of the girls was looking adoringly at Randy. This one she didn't know. The girl on the other side was Pris Gosling. Her eyes were on Brew alone.

Robin felt her face grow hot. While Cass was crying in the doctor's office, Brew was not only winning honor and glory in the golf tournament but was being admired by the dreadful, predatory Pris as he did it! It was shameful! It was not fair! Saying the words aloud, however, forced a small note of reason to intervene. Just because I can't stand Brew, she thought, it isn't right to blame him unfairly. Cass had not told Brew she'd been sick. She had not told him that she was going to the doctor. Nor the reason. Brew loved Cass or he would not have let happen what did happen. Because Brew loved Cass he would want to marry her. If you did not believe that, what could you believe?

As for Pris Gosling being there, Pris was her own boss. She did what she wanted. Not that this rationalization about Brew or Pris made it any easier for Cass. Cass was the one who was trapped. She was the one who had to make the admission of guilt to her parents. How would a person do it? Where would a girl begin? How could she explain? I would die, Robin thought.

She walked over to the window. On the sidewalk in front of the house a little girl was pushing a doll carriage up and down. A lump came in Robin's throat. She turned and walked slowly down the stairs.

A. R. "Curly" Carter. The name stared up at her. Robin had never known any other fathers who had their nicknames in the phone book.

She dialed the number. The ringing stopped. A child's high-pitched voice said "hello."

Robin's "May I speak to Cass, please," was followed by a clatter and bang as the receiver at the other end of the wire fell to the floor. The child's diminishing voice cried out, "Cass, it's for you."

Robin moved the phone to her other hand, took a deep breath. She had not known she would be so nervous.

There was the sound of heavy footsteps approaching and Robin's palms grew moist. "This is Cass's father. What do you want?"

"To . . . to talk to Cass."

"She's not here."

The connection was broken almost before the last word had sounded.

Robin stared at the lifeless receiver. If Cass was not there, why had the child who answered said, "Cass, it's for you."

Between classes on Monday, Robin searched the corridors for the flash of Cass's bright hair but she did not see her as she sometimes did. At lunch, Judy, to whom Robin had confided everything, could only say that she hadn't seen Cass either but that didn't mean she wasn't at school. "Even with our lockers right next to each other, sometimes our paths just don't cross at all."

Brew, however, was very much in evidence. Flushed with his golf victory, he was in the center of first one admiring little cluster and then another.

"Sycophants," Judy said, sternly. "*We* come to bury Caesar, not praise him" and tromped off to class.

The girls did not meet again until after school when Judy conceded that Cass had not been at school. "After I left you today noon, I went back to my locker hoping Cass would show up. While I was there, Ginny Park came by. 'If you're waiting for Cass,' she said, 'don't. She's home. Sick.' She said the word 'Sick' in that particularly nasty, irritating way she has. I wonder if she knows anything."

"I don't see how she could," Robin began, "unless..."

"Unless what?"

"Unless Tina Sellers could have told her. I saw Tina when we were in the dime store buying the wedding ring, but I didn't think Tina saw us. And even if she did, how could she put two and two together?"

"Don't ask me." Judy sounded so cross that Robin decided to let the matter drop. If she, herself, thought about Cass any more her head would split. And it was probably pointless anyway. Cass would be back at school the next day. After all, only three weeks remained until graduation and with final exams and papers due, practice for the senior play and arrangements for Class Day, she could not afford to miss.

Holding her hands under the hot-air dryer in the girls' rest room, Robin did not hear any of the conversation of the two girls standing several lavatories away until the blower she was using shut itself off.

PART TWO: *Cass*

"I hear Cass Carter got herself in trouble," the tall, thin one said. She tossed her long, lanky, and not-too-clean hair out of her eyes as she spoke.

"Yeah?" The other girl stopped putting on lipstick long enough to stare at her companion. "Who's the guy?"

"Who knows? The crowd she runs around with, it could be anybody."

"That's not true!"

Both girls turned at the same time, eyes staring, mouths agape, each so busy with character assassination that they had not noticed when Robin approached them.

The thin, lank-haired one was the first to pull herself together. "Yeah? And what do *you* know about it?"

"Yeah," said the other. "What do *you* know about it?"

"Because I know Cass! That's why." Robin's voice shook.

"If you're so smart," said lank-hair, "I suppose you know that she's not going to graduate, either. If you don't believe me, just look in Mrs. Dempsey's office. They've just posted the list of graduates on the bulletin board. Cass Carter's name isn't there. Come, Gloria."

Numbly, Robin watched them go. It was true that almost the whole week had gone by and Cass had not returned to school. Twice, when she'd tried to talk to Cass at home, Mr. Carter had answered the phone. Each time, hearing Robin's voice, he'd hung up without saying a word. On one occasion she'd reached Mrs. Carter, but that phone call had been no more satisfactory than the others.

"I'm sorry . . . Cass's father . . . He doesn't like to have me talk about it. I'm afraid I have to go now . . ." and the connection was broken so gently that seconds passed before Robin could be sure that no one was there.

Robin's footsteps resounded lonesomely as she went down the corridor toward Mrs. Dempsey's office and pushed through the door marked Girls' Advisor.

The list was neatly typed on four pages, two columns of names to the page, and thumb-tacked to the pock-marked and punctured bulletin board just outside Mrs. Dempsey's office. Robin's vision blurred as she read through the list of the B's and the beginning of the C's. Brinkman, Bywater, Cameron, Capps, Clanghorn, Critchfield, Crowly, Czardas. She read them through again. Cass's name was not there.

The door to Mrs. Dempsey's office was open and Mrs. Dempsey was seated at her desk. She looked up just as Robin turned from the bulletin board and for the briefest instant their eyes met.

Should she go marching in and point out the omission to Mrs. Dempsey? Or would it be better to wait until Monday? Perhaps by then the mistake would have been discovered and Cass's name would be neatly lettered in between Capps and Clanghorn.

She turned away, walked slowly down the corridor to the English classroom where Judy was making up a test that she had missed the day before. Furrowing her brow, concentrating on Judy, Robin ordered Judy to look up.

Rather to Robin's surprise—for her, this trick of furrowing and concentrating learned from Judy seldom worked—Judy did look up.

Robin gestured, mouthed her message, and pointed in the direction of home.

Judy gestured "Go away." Her eyes returned to the paper on which she had been writing and although Robin concentrated and furrowed like everything she could not make Judy look up again.

She sighed. There was no use waiting. She hoisted the armload of books to a more comfortable position and pushed through the heavy door into the outside freshness of the May day, but it did little for her spirit. In fact, she was so wrapped up in Cass's problems that she had walked more than a block before she was aware of the sound of pounding feet behind her and someone yelling hoarsely. Robin stopped and turned around.

It was Judy, breathless and a little splotchy from running. "When I waved at you to go away," Judy panted, "I didn't mean for you to *clear* away. Mrs. Bird had left me on my honor while I wrote the test and I was afraid she might come back and think you were signalling me an answer." Judy paused, took a tremendous swallow of air. "The worst thing just happened now. You'd never guess!"

"If you mean about Cass's name not being on the senior list, I know. That's what I was to tell you. But it's a mistake. It has to be."

"It's no mistake." Judy's eyes, round and brown as pennies could not conceal her superior knowledge. "After I finished the test, I went to get my sweater out of my locker. Cass's locker was standing open. And of all the stuff she had crammed in there, there's nothing left. Not a single thing."

4

"Thank you, but no thanks," Judy said.

"Well, if you won't go with me, I'll go alone."

Judy shook her head. "Go right ahead. But I'd be afraid. What if her father's home?"

"He can't do any more than shut the door in my face." Indignation made Robin sound braver than she really felt. "And after all, he might not even be there. The last time I called, whatever day it was, it was right after school and her mother answered. He might be on a new shift or something."

"I'm chicken and you might as well face it," Judy said cheerfully. "After all, you told me yourself that Cass was afraid of him. She said he'd kill her if he found out."

"I know." Robin shivered in spite of herself. "But that was just talk. He didn't mean it. She didn't mean it. He's really awfully proud of her. She's getting a watch, one of those good kind you don't have to wind, for graduation."

"I'd rather do without the watch and have a different father."

The argument was unanswerable. In the end, Robin went to Cass's house alone.

It had been easy to lay the ground. "I'll be kind of late getting home," she had told her mother when she left that morning. And her mother, busy with a new project, had cheerfully said, "Have a nice day, darling," and that was all.

Having a nice day, however, did not necessarily mean doing happy things. It could mean doing things that you ought to do. Going to see Cass was in the latter category. Cass had been her friend. Was her friend. If Cass ever needed her, it was now.

Waiting for the bus, Robin's face grew hot with shame as she thought of the way Cass had been talked about. Although only a week had passed since the list of graduating seniors had been posted, gossip had spread throughout the school. Everybody knew everything, yet no one knew anything.

The corridors buzzed with "Have you heards," voices

dropping as the news about Cass went forth. Eyes widened, breath was excitedly drawn in. There were snickers and nervous laughter. Sometimes there was shocked, unbelieving silence. Some said she was coming back to graduate with her class. Others said she had dropped out for good.

A few said, "Poor Cass." Some, like Tina Sellers, with hardened sophistication, said, "Lots of kids do what Cass did. She got caught—that's all." A couple of kids had got caught the year before. But they had been nobodies. They had vanished from school and it hadn't mattered. Cass did. Mattered, at least, as a topic of conversation to almost everybody but Linda Summers who, for a while, had been Cass's best friend.

"I don't want to talk about it," Linda said one day that week when Robin sought her out. She gave a little shudder. "It's too terrible."

"I thought maybe Cass had called you," Robin said, a little apologetically. "It's just that I'd like to know how she is ... what's happening at her house."

"Well, she hasn't called me," Linda said in a quite different tone, "and frankly, I hope she doesn't. It would upset my mother, for one thing. And for another thing, I've got my own reputation to think of. I just wouldn't want to be seen with her, if you know what I mean— pregnant and all."

"But as soon as she and Brew are married, then everything will be all right."

"As soon as she and Brew are married!" Linda's laugh was short and brittle. "That will be the day."

"But they will!" Robin cried. "He . . . he wants to. He'll have to marry Cass. It wouldn't be fair if he didn't."

Linda shook her head almost pityingly. "You are a baby! Don't you know that what is right and what is fair doesn't have anything to do with it?"

Linda Summers was a smart girl and a senior class officer, but she could not be right about Brew and Cass. Although life for Brew was going on as before, he could not be blamed for that. He could still love Cass and want to marry her, even if Pris Gosling and other goose-girls did persist in hanging around. He was the kind of boy who would always enjoy admiration.

On the bus there was no chance to think at all. The route it traveled was unfamiliar, and wedged in as she was among the noisy, jostling standees it was difficult to recognize the corner where she thought she should get off. But she did, ringing the bell just in time, finding herself very near the place she had exited from the freeway the day she had driven Cass home. Scarcely two months had passed since then, yet it seemed almost a lifetime ago.

That day it had been cold and windy. Now the trees were leafed out in tenderest green. The breeze was soft and a fat robin chirped "Cheer up, cheerily" from a gnarled lilac bush. It was a day meant for being outdoors. The street was alive with children, trundling up and down on tricycles, playing ball or hopscotch or jacks, making mud pies.

Some of the children were bound to be Carters. She thought she might recognize Louis, the brother she'd seen delivering papers the day she brought Cass home. But of Louis she saw no sign.

Next door to the Carters' house, however, two small boys sat side by side on the curbing. One was a thin, dark child with eyes the color of ripe olives. The other was fair-skinned. His hair was the same bright red-gold shade as Cass's.

Robin stopped. "Hi."

Both little boys looked up.

Robin addressed the bright-haired one. "Is your daddy home today?"

His gaze was solemn and appraising. "Kirkie wets," he said.

Robin smiled and sighed at the same time. There wasn't going to be any easy way to find out if Cass's father would be home. The only solution was to march firmly up to the front door, knock, and say, "May I please speak to Cass?"

Even if Mr. Carter came to the door, even if he was brusque and gruff and did not invite her in, still Cass would know that she had been there; that she had not been forgotten.

Robin found two pennies in her purse, gave one to

A Girl Like Me

each child and walked on. She could feel the children's
eyes upon her as she turned up the cindered drive to the
house. A pot of straggly geraniums bloomed bravely by
the front step. In the side yard, a washing flapped from a
wire clothesline.

Robin's heart pounded as the knocker fell. Judy had
been right all along. It had been madness to come. It was
all she could do to keep from running.

The door opened. Robin looked down into the eyes of
a little girl of nine or ten.

"My name is Robin. Is your sister, Cass, at home?"
The words came out in a little rush, her relief was so
great.

The little girl's half-fearful expression faded. She
smiled timidly, then without answering sped on bare silent feet upstairs.

The room in which Robin stood was shabby, sparsely
furnished but pin-neat. The floors were waxed and
shiny, the curtains clean and starchy. Through an open
window the sound of children playing drifted in. A
moment later she heard light footsteps descending the
stair.

The woman who came toward her had once looked
like Cass, Robin thought. She felt the pang of omnis-
cience. Once Mrs. Carter had also been fair and rosy.
Now she was pallid, her eyes dark-circled; her hair was
dulled with gray. Like a shadow the little girl who had
opened the door to Robin came edging along behind
her.

Mrs. Carter turned. "Run along, Mavis, and look after the little ones. Mother wants to talk to Cass's friend alone." Her voice was gentle and the child left reluctantly.

"I . . . I'm Robin James." As she spoke, she had an almost overwhelming desire to fling herself, weeping, into the arms of this woman whose own eyes showed the signs of recent tears.

"I'm glad you came. Cass spoke of you often. She . . . she would have called you, if she could."

Robin's heart gave an unpleasant leaden thump. Mrs. Carter spoke of Cass as if she were dead! Why did she not call Cass—it was Cass that she had come to see—then go away so they could have a few minutes alone together.

Mrs. Carter glanced quickly, nervously over her shoulder. "You must forgive me. But Cass's father has taken it so terribly hard. He . . . we had such hopes for her." Tears began to creep down her cheeks as she spoke. "I don't know whether or not Cass told you, but somehow . . . somehow we'd hoped to manage college for her. She would have had to work part-time, of course, but it would have meant so much. For her future. For . . . us. You see, no one in her father's family or my family had ever gone before . . ."

Robin stared down at her hands, blinking hard to hold back her own tears.

With an effort Mrs. Carter straightened her shoulders then broke into quiet controlled sobbing. "But I could have stood that. I could have stood someone else taking her part in the senior play. Or not graduating with her class. If only . . . if only we hadn't had to send her away . . ."

For a moment Robin could not breathe at all. "Send her away? What do you mean? I . . . I don't understand . . ."

"Cass's father. He's a proud man. He stood it for a week, then he couldn't take it any more . . . seeing her every day . . . seeing her so pitiful and sick. Not able to go to school. Everyone in the neighborhood knowing. I don't know how they knew, but they did."

Once again the furtive almost frightened look came into Mrs. Carter's eyes. "H . . . her father made me promise not to tell, but soon everyone will know it anyway. We took her this morning to the Mission Hospital for unmarried mothers."

5

Without the car, Robin would never have attempted to find Cass. Even with the car, it was turning into a seemingly hopeless quest.

Before she left home, she pored over a map of the city but it was drawn on such a scale that the street on which the Mission Hospital was located appeared only as an infinitesimal line—one of a dozen or more infinitesimal lines that fanned out from an intersection of thorough-fares. Now it had all vanished from her head. In fact, the section of the city where she found herself—the older part—history books said it had its beginning when the fur traders moved up the Mississippi—was so unfamiliar that she no longer knew in which direction she was going.

A block or so down the street on which she was rather aimlessly headed, she could see a flurry of small red and blue plastic pennants flying around a gas station. Gas station people were good at giving directions. She'd had no luck a little while before. Then, when she'd stopped the car and asked a grandmotherly-looking woman who was walking by to direct her to the Mission Hospital, the woman had just shook her head and hurried on her way.

This gas station, however, was not the nicest looking one Robin had ever seen. Nor was the boy who came slouching out of the small frame building the nicest looking boy. The name "Orval" was written in faded blue thread on his dirty coverall. He leaned an elbow in the car's open window and grinned. "What can I do you for? Gasoline, air for your tires, or do you just want to pass the time of day?"

"I . . . could you . . ." She flushed, aware that with this boy she was not sure how to go on.

"Spill it, kiddo. I won't eat you." His breath, as he leaned toward her, was an unpleasant mixture of spearmint and stale tobacco.

"I'm looking for the Mission Hospital." She blurted out the words in a voice that held both defiance and apology. "I . . . I guess I'm lost."

"Yeah? You know something?" The boy's face was

now peering in the window. "You don't look the type, somehow." Robin felt his glance sliding over her like an oily film."

"I . . . I'm going to see a friend."

"Yeah?"

The single word, spoken in a tone of mocking disbelief, was followed by a false, yapping laugh.

In a fury, Robin shoved the Volksie into gear almost running over the toe of the attendant's dirty tennis shoe. She didn't care. With scarcely a glance in either direction she darted into the stream of traffic, missed an oncoming truck by inches. At the next corner she made a sudden right turn and there, before her anger had a chance to cool, she saw the sign. It was inconspicuous, discreetly lettered MISSION HOSPITAL.

The long drive was tree-bordered. The building, too, for all its size seemed to be cloaked in a protective covering so that, had she not been looking for it, it would have been almost invisible from the street.

Robin pulled into a parking area labeled "Visitors." She was filled with a nervous foreboding. Now, for the first time, she wished that she had let Judy come with her. Judy had wanted to, terribly. But to Robin it did not seem right. "You wouldn't go with me to Cass's house when I wanted you to," she said, "and I don't think you ought to see her now—almost as if she's on exhibit."

Judy had looked embarrassed but was frank about it.

"Well, going to her house if her father was there, would have been nerve-wracking. But going to see her in the hospital—a hospital like the one where she is—that would be psychologically interesting."

Robin put on the short white gloves she'd brought with her, then took them off. She wished she knew what time it was—she'd wasted almost an hour driving around—and she'd promised her mother to be back at four o'clock. But, at least, there'd been no questions asked about where she was going. If there had been, she would have said she was going to see Cass. Which was the truth—as far as it went.

She got out of the car and took a deep breath to make her heart slow its pace. As she walked toward the building a station wagon passed her, stopping in front of the entrance. A man got out, lifted a suitcase over the tailgate. As he stood waiting, the weight pulled at his arm, adding further to his attitude of dejection. A sad-faced woman and a girl with eyes red from crying got out of the car and joined them. The girl looked younger than Cass. The three of them trailed up the steps, then the man put the suitcase down while the girl clung to him and cried before turning to cling to the woman.

Robin turned away, wiping away tears that she could not hold back with the finger of her glove. Not until the man and woman had gone back to their car and driven away did Robin go inside the building. The girl had disappeared. A pleasant-looking woman with gray hair

PART TWO: *Cass*

looked up from the small switchboard where she sat. "May I help you?"

Robin nodded. "I have a friend. Her name is Cass Carter. May I see her, please?"

"Just a moment." A light flashed on the switchboard, the woman released a connection, made another. "Matron," she said discreetly. "One of the girls has a caller."

Robin perched uneasily on the edge of her chair wondering which of the three doors in the room would open. A moment later, Robin felt herself shrinking. The spare, yet strongly-built woman who looked down at her almost filled the doorway in which she stood. She had iron-gray hair and iron-gray eyes. There was even a faint grayish pallor to her skin. All else, her nurse's uniform, hose, and shoes were of a spotless white.

Robin shut her eyes, swallowed but when no sound came forth the woman at the switchboard intervened with a little smile. "She would like to see Cass Carter, Matron."

"There's nothing to be afraid of." The tall, gray woman's tone was dry but not unkind. "If you will just wait for a moment, I'll find out if your friend would like to see you. You must understand that while we are willing for our girls to have visitors, the girls themselves are not always willing to see them. Your name?"

"Robin James. She . . . Cass goes to the same school . . . went to the same school . . . I do."

"I see," the Matron said. She was smiling faintly.

Soundlessly, she disappeared through a door other than the one by which she had entered and after what seemed like eons later, as soundlessly reappeared.

"Please, come with me."

Robin followed the straight back of the Matron down a long hall. Through a half-open door Robin could see into one of the rooms. A row of cots was lined up against a wall. A girl, wearing a dark skirt and short white smock, lay on her back on one of them. Her hands were clasped behind her head and she was staring at the ceiling.

The iron-gray woman tapped at several closed doors, opened them and looked in. Each time, however, she closed them so quickly that Robin could not see inside.

When she paused again it was to say, "This is one of the rooms where our girls receive visitors. You may wait here. Your friend will be along soon." She went away.

The room held a sofa covered with a paisley throw, several straight-backed chairs, and a small table. A clean ash tray was on the table and a small pot of tired ivy.

Too nervous to sit still, Robin tiptoed to the door and looked down the corridor. From somewhere she could hear the faint sound of crying. Maybe it was the new girl she had just seen arrive. Perhaps it was Cass. Cass was quite a new girl, too.

As Robin stood in the doorway, she saw a boy come toward her. Hands thrust deep into his pockets, shoulders hunched, he did not see her as he walked past. She went back in the room, parted the limp gauzy curtain at the single window and stared out into the back yard of the hospital where a long row of white smocks and dark skirts hung from a clothesline. At a sound behind her, she turned.

It was Cass. She was pale, thinner than when Robin had gone with her to see Dr. Munzinger. When was it? Two, almost three weeks ago? Her face had the finely-honed look of one who has long been ill. But even at a glance Robin could see that Cass was not the one who had been crying. She was wearing a dark skirt and white smock like those Robin had seen on the clothesline.

"So you decided to see how the Outcast of Poker Flat was getting along?" Cass said.

Robin flushed. The story, one by Bret Harte, was on the outside reading list for Junior English. Cass knew that she knew what it was about: that its principal characters were a gambler, a drunkard, and two women of bad reputation who were expelled from a Western mining camp. It was not fair for Cass to start the conversation like this and if a small, sardonic smile had not hovered about her mouth, Robin would have left without saying a word. But pity filled her.

"I went to your house and talked to your mother. She said you were here. I wanted to come before, but you know how it is . . ." Robin's eyes fell. Cass, still silent, still wearing the same unamused smile, was not making it easy to go on. "The last couple of weeks of school are awfully busy." Robin stopped abruptly. She should not have said that. It was something she had vowed not to do—make any reference to school at all.

"They've had the senior play, haven't they?"

Robin nodded.

Cass stared down at her hands, fingers spread upon her knees, then put them behind her. "Who did . . . Mr. Gartner . . . give my part to?"

"Tina Sellers," Robin said with a little gulp. "She wasn't any good." The words tripped the little trigger that had held her in control. "I left when it was half over. I couldn't stand it—seeing her in your part." She dug in her purse for a handkerchief, noisily blew her nose. "*I* shouldn't be crying. As bad as I feel, I know you feel a thousand times worse. Not being in the play . . . missing the senior prom . . . and worst of all, not graduating . . ."

"I'm graduating," Cass said coldly.

"How can you? I mean, when you're not going to school?"

"Don't be naive," Cass said with a brittle little laugh. "Of course, I'm graduating. I'll be getting a diploma just like everybody else in my class, except I won't be marching up on the stage at the Civic Center in a cap and gown to get it. We'll have our ceremony here. A nice selective little ceremony here in the cafeteria. Just the six of us. It's really quite cosmopolitan. We've girls from all over the state."

Robin felt a constriction around her heart as she

looked at Cass. It would be better for Cass to cry than to talk like this.

"While there are only six in our graduating class, quite a lot more go to school here. The teacher is really very nice. She's been here twenty years. The social worker's nice, too. They try to help you. They try to understand. Which is more than your own father will do." Cass laughed again, a tinkling, ice-cold laugh. "Your own father, for instance, won't talk to you at all!"

"Cass, don't. Please!"

"I don't see why you're upset," Cass said. "I like it here. They're not too strict. You can go downtown. You can have callers. Of course, when your mother comes she cries all the time which makes it just dandy. But otherwise . . ." She shrugged. "Sometimes, even boys come. Come for a while, that is. After a few visits, they find it depressing. Depressing! Imagine that!" Cass trilled falsely. "In any case, most of them stop coming before very long."

"Oh, no!" Robin cried. She put her hand to her throat to stop the hurt. "Brew wouldn't stop coming!"

"Brew? If you mean Brewster Bailey Winfield, the Third, he's never come at all. I thought you knew! I thought everybody knew! Why else would I be here in this . . . in this . . . place."

"But I thought . . . I mean, just as soon as school is out and Brew graduates, then you and he will be getting married . . ."

"Married! You are a dummy! Almost as big a dummy

as I was to believe that Brew meant it when he said he loved me . . ." For the first time, Cass's voice faltered. "We were going to wait until fall, though; wait until Brew had started to college and pledged a fraternity. I was going to work during the day and just take some night classes myself until he finished. We . . . we thought it would work out."

"I still don't understand . . . What happened? When . . ."

"Oh, it happened right away. He didn't waste any time at all." Cass's voice now had a put-on brightness. "I didn't think I'd see him that Saturday night, but I did. He got back from the golf tournament sooner than he expected. I was glad I hadn't said anything to my folks. I thought everything would turn out all right. We drove down to the old covered bridge near Amity Falls. It's pretty there. There was a moon. And we had a lot to talk about. He was on high because he'd won the golf tournament that day. But when I told him that I'd been feeling sick and had gone to the doctor, and that we'd have to get married sooner than we thought—maybe right away, or as soon as school was out—he took his arm away . . ." Cass began speaking more slowly, with a little pause between each word as if she had to visualize the scene before she described it. "He . . . took . . . his . . . arm . . . away . . . and just stared down the valley. Then . . . he said, in this matter-of-fact voice, 'We can't get married now. You know that. It would be better to get rid of the kid. There are doctors who do that sort of thing.' "

Cass looked at Robin. Her eyes had the opaque, unseeing look of the blind. "Even if I lost Brew, I knew I couldn't have an abortion. I guess I got pretty hysterical, but it didn't help. Brew drove me around until I'd quieted down, then he took me home. After that, there wasn't anything to do but tell my mother. I told her that night. She told my father. I thought at first he might kill me. Instead, he sent me here." Like a sleepwalker suddenly awakening, Cass returned to reality and once again her voice reflected her bitterness. "Mr. Winfield's in New York now, but when he gets back my father is going to threaten him to make Brew marry me. But that'll be a waste of time. Even if Brew would, I wouldn't. Nobody has to marry me! Nobody!"

"But the baby . . ." Robin faltered.

"Let someone else worry about the baby. I've worries enough of my own."

"You're not going to keep it?"

"Keep it!" Cass cried. "Of course, I'm not going to keep it!" Her laugh was high, strained, now almost uncontrollable. "If everybody kept her baby, where would *you* be? Answer me that! Just what kind of a life do you suppose you would have had, if your mother had kept you?"

Robin's eyes widened, stared at Cass who seemed to crumble as she looked at her.

"I didn't mean it!" Cass cried. She knelt at Robin's feet. "I take it back! I didn't mean it. Forgive me. Say you forgive me."

Woodenly, Robin got to her feet.

"Don't go!" Cass dragged at her hand. Tears were running down her cheeks. "I don't know why I said that . . . you . . . my only friend."

Robin walked away from Cass's restraining hands, down the corridor. Her feet moved her forward in a stiff-jointed, robot-like step.

When the woman at the switchboard said "good-bye," she did not answer for she did not hear.

PART THREE

Francie

I

That evening there were candles on the table. It was set with the best silver and the Waterford crystal that had belonged to Irish great-grandmother Tuhill who had still been "full of herself" at ninety.

A celebration, Mrs. James said, in honor of Robin's father who had been lost in his laboratory for almost a week. Things had not been going well with the grass-hoppers at all.

Mrs. James had fixed the dishes Mr. James liked best. They were Robin's favorites, too—but it was only by cutting her food into the smallest bites that she could swallow at all.

Her father, relaxed and happy, had wet down his hair as a small boy does before coming to the table. Thick, curly, and with a mind of its own, it was already humping into its usual bumpy waves. Her mother's cheeks were pink from the heat of the kitchen and her dark eyes reflected the candlelight.

Robin put down her fork and looked away from the hypnotic glittering of the flames. The "conversation" was starting again. She could not stop it. The words, lying long forgotten at the bottom of her mind, were as sharp and clear as if they had been spoken but the day before.

There were pictures, too. She could see herself as she'd been then: sitting beneath the Christmas tree, a tree so tall that the star on the top brushed the ceiling.

"I'm so glad we adopted you!" Arms were wrapped around her in a warm embrace. "You're our darling adopted baby," her father said. "Before we adopted you, we only had a little teeny, weeny Christmas tree," said her mother.

And there she was with Robinson, the teddy bear who was every bit as big as she. She was sitting on him, on the floor. The whirring sound grew louder in her brain.

"Every little girl has a mama who carries her, when she is a tiny baby, inside her body until she is born. But sometimes, something happens to the mama so that she can't keep her baby and take care of her. So she finds another mama and daddy who don't have any little girl,

and are oh, so sad and lonely for one, and they are hunting for one. And the first mama gives them her little girl
and they are so glad to have a little girl! And the first
mama is glad, too, because her little girl has someone
who will love and take care of her."

"Did I grow in your tummy?" She was older then.

"No, you grew in the tummy of another lady."

"Then, do I have two mothers?"

"You were born from your first mother. I am your
second mother. I am your always mother."

"Robin!" her father said.

She jerked herself to attention. The voices faded and
were gone.

Her father was smiling. "You were about a million
miles away. Your mother was speaking to you."

"I was just saying that Sam came over this afternoon.
We really talked! He's a nice boy, Robin."

By buttering a piece of roll and putting it in her
mouth, Robin made a nod suffice.

"I think what he really wanted," her mother went on,
"was to find out if you were still going out with Randy.
I said 'no.'" She waited. "He said he hardly ever sees
you at school."

"We don't have any classes together," Robin muttered. She sensed, though she could not see, the invisible
exchange of glances that passed between her parents.

"I think he'd ask you out tonight if he thought you'd
go."

"I'd better study." She tried to sound regretful but it was no use. Sam belonged to her childhood and that was a lifetime ago.

Her mother looked across at Robin's plate. "Maybe it's the end of semester syndrome, but you're not eating anything at all."

"It . . . it's delicious. I'm just not terribly hungry."

"Too many tests," her father said. "I think they work the kids too hard."

Her mother looked sympathetic. "If you'd like to be excused," she said, "you may."

Robin said thank you and pushed back her chair. There was a beading of perspiration under her bangs. She walked carefully, holding herself very straight. Her feet seemed very far away.

Slowly, Robin climbed the stairs to her room. The voices were silent now. She made no attempt to study but stared down at her desk, not seeing the books she'd brought home the day before nor the unfinished English theme assigned a week ago that was due on Monday.

If Judy had not told Cass she was adopted, Cass would never have spoken the words that brought her to the threshold of a door that never before had been opened.

But Judy had told. Tears smarted in Robin's eyes. "My friend," she said. "Some friend." She'd found out it was Judy that day when, late as it was, she stopped at Harts on her way home from Mission Hospital. Judy, who'd been digging dandelions in the front yard, came over to the car and when Robin questioned her admitted it at once. It had come up, she confessed, when Cass had once said something about Robin looking like her mother.

"I told her it was just a coincidence that you looked alike, because you were adopted." Judy had flushed to the roots of her ginger-colored hair. "I wouldn't have told her if I'd thought you'd care," then almost defensively had added, "You didn't used to."

Didn't used to! Of course, she didn't "used to"! But there was a difference in how you felt when you were six and bragged about being the prettiest little baby in the Child Jesus Home, and how you felt when you were sixteen.

None of her newer friends knew she was adopted. Not that it was any secret. She just didn't tell. Some of the kids she'd met since she started to senior high even kidded her about inherited traits! "No wonder Rob's so good in biology," Liz Larkin, who'd been her lab partner the year before, said with good-natured envy. "She's inherited all those scientific brains from her father. And you know how smart *he* is."

If someone commented on how much she reminded them of one parent or another, she'd made a point of not setting them right. She didn't deny it. She just kept still.

Robin switched off the light and threw herself across the bed without undressing, pressed her hot cheek to the cool pillow. Once, a long time ago, Judy said that burying things in your mind didn't do any good at all. That no matter how deeply they lay, if you pretended they weren't there, they could do you harm. Sigmund Freud had figured it out, she explained, and a Freudian psychiatrist was what she intended to be.

The voices and the pictures were once again whirring in her brain. Why should the prompt and casual answer to a childish question asked in the long ago be coming back to her now?

Had it been too prompt? Too casual?

"I didn't know your first mother and daddy," her mother said. "There are lots of reasons why a lady and a man might not be able to keep their baby. I'm sure they had a very good reason."

Robin turned over on her back and in the darkness dug her knuckles into her closed eyes until showers of color, crazy shapes of crimson, purple and green, exploded behind her closed lids.

A very good reason? What *kind* of reason? A reason, she whispered, that *I* should know?

There was a step in the hall outside her door. A light, listening step. "Mama?" Robin said.

The door opened and her mother was silhouetted in a rectangle of melon-colored light.

"You're not asleep?"

It was not really a question and Robin did not answer. Her mother crossed the room and sat down in a rocking chair beside the bed. The mothering chair, her mother called it, because it was just the right height and size for a mother to rock her baby in. Or her little girl.

"We must have rocked a million miles," her mother once had said. She didn't need to be told that. She remembered, could not forget, the fiery boring pain of the earaches that had tormented her until she was almost seven. When she'd had her adenoids and tonsils out, the earaches had disappeared but even after that, whenever she was sick, they had rocked until her mother was almost submerged beneath her in the little chair.

Her mother leaned her head back against the rocker. Though Robin could not see her eyes she knew that they were shut. "These first days of almost-summer *do* make one tired. I think it would be a good idea if everyone in this family went to bed early and got a good night's rest."

The words Robin had thought were forming on her lips—something about studying better early next morning—were never spoken. "Why did my first mother give me up?" she said.

The whispering of the rocker ceased and there was silence in the room.

"Why, I don't really know," her mother said. She spoke slowly, in a careful measured way.

If it were not for the darkness, Robin thought, I could see her face. Then I would know if she was telling the truth. She felt cold, dispassionate, outside herself. She had not intended to ask the question. It had come surging up out of the dark, sunken rivers of her mind, and now it must be answered.

"The agency may have told us something about your first parents, but it's so long ago that I can't remember the exact details. There are a number of reasons babies are given up for adoption. Sometimes it is because of death or illness. Sometimes it is divorce that breaks up a family circle so that the child needs a new family to be his very own."

The rocking chair had resumed its gentle whispering. Downstairs, rifle shots rang out as her father tuned in on his favorite western TV show. Her mother's voice went on, more slowly, more carefully than before.

"I'm sure your mother's reason was a good one. Perhaps, her reason was the best one of all—she simply felt she could not give you a happy home. We do know that the people at the adoption agency must have thought she made a wise decision because they helped her carry out her wish to have you adopted. And they placed you with us because they felt we were very much alike." Mrs. James' voice changed from thoughtful to the one which sometimes made Robin laugh. "*One* way in which we're very much alike is that we could go on talking half the night." Briskly, she got to her feet. "Only this time, *I'm* doing all the talking." She leaned over the bed, felt for Robin's face with both her kind hands. "You'll go to bed soon, though, won't you? O.K.?"

Robin's lips touched her mother's cheek. She murmured "good night" and faked a casual yawn. She felt only a moment's guiltiness at her deceit. For a child, the tale her mother had told might be enough. But not for her. She had to know more—who she was and where she came from, and what kind of a mother gave her birth— and then had given her away.

2

When Robin's father offered her a ride downtown the first day after school was out, she accepted without a twinge of conscience. After all, she reminded herself, she *was* looking for a job. Looking for a job was not the *only* thing she was going to do that day.

Her father grinned reassuringly as he dropped her at the bank corner. "Don't worry if you don't get that job. We aren't going to charge you room and board for a while yet."

Robin grinned back. "I'm glad to hear it. At least fifty other kids filled out applications for this one messenger job last January. And as far as I know, all fifty were asked to come back when school was out. I've got a couple of other places I'm going to investigate, though, so don't give up hope."

She slammed the door smartly, then stood for a moment on the sidewalk until her father's car vanished in the maze of traffic. A mirror was set into the window of the jewelry store that adjoined the bank and seeing herself there she nodded at her reflection, politely, as one might do to a pretty stranger. Her hair being up did make a difference—though it had taken every little comb, clip, bobby pin, and hairpin she could lay her hands on to anchor it in the proper place. Hose and heels added to a grown-up effect she could hardly help but admire. A bit more lipstick would make her look older still which fortunately was as important for job hunting as it was for what she called, to herself, "the other."

Robin found lipstick and was leaning toward the mirror to apply it when a cheerful, familiar voice behind her said, "Go ahead and put some more on but it won't do any good. I just came from the bank. The job's filled."

The speaker was Paula Bemis, a girl Robin liked but did not know well. "The messenger job, I mean," Paula said, "if that's where you're headed."

"I was," Robin said. "I didn't have any great hope of getting it though. Oh, well . . . I have a couple of other prospects."

Paula's grin spread still wider. "Tell me where you're going and maybe I can save you some time and energy. I got an earlier start this morning than you did."

Robin produced a clipping of the "help wanted" column from the newspaper. It was identical with the one Paula Bemis held. "Let me see . . . the Burgett Company. File clerk?"

Paula shook her head. "Filled."

"Breen Brothers. Clerk."

"Filled."

"Marasco and Sons. Stock girl."

"I could have had that one. If I'd lied. But they didn't want to hire anyone who would be going back to school this fall."

"That would let me out, too." Robin wadded the strip of news print into a little ball. "That's it, then, I guess. Back to baby-sitting."

"I've one more lead," Paula said, "but if I told you, you might get it instead of me."

"Good luck," Robin said, "and thanks for saving me all that running around. See you next fall. 'Bye." She did not want to sound impatient, but now that job-hunting was taken care of for the day she couldn't wait for Paula to be gone. All during the preceding week she'd barely allowed herself to think about it at all. But now exams were over. School was out. A little later when a bus headed in the proper direction came lumbering down the street, Robin got on. The adventure that perhaps would lead to discovery was about to begin.

"Department of vital statistics, third floor, elevator to your right."

Her heart beating pleasantly with excitement, Robin followed the directions given. The girl at the information desk in the lobby of the big limestone building had not even looked up! Robin took this as a good sign. There must be nothing unusual at all about asking where one went to get a copy of one's birth certificate.

The department of vital statistics, however, turned out to look not at all as she had imaged. True, the building in which it was housed was almost new but it did seem that any office that dealt with marriage, birth, and death records should be filled with musty filing cabinets and mouldering old leather volumes. Here, everything looked efficient and modern. Beyond the counter at which she stood there were a dozen or more desks, at each of which a girl or woman sat busily typing. A middle-aged, pleasant-looking woman at the nearest desk got up when she saw Robin.

"May I help you?"

Reassured, Robin returned her smile. "I'd like a copy of my birth certificate, please."

The woman reached beneath the counter to take a paper from the shelf. "You're going traveling, I expect. An exchange student?"

"Pardon me?"

"Oh, perhaps not. I thought you might be going as an exchange student from one of our high schools to a foreign country. A birth certificate is needed for passport purposes, you know."

Robin shook her head. The palms of her hands had grown a little moist. "No. Not that."

"Whatever the reason—school entrance, social security, employment—it doesn't matter," the woman said soothingly. "Just fill out this form. There is a fee of one dollar, however, which is required by law when we search our files for a vital record."

"Oh, that will be all right." Robin could not keep the relief from her voice. Though she had not known it would cost anything, she had foresightedly brought money along.

She picked up the ballpoint pen on the counter and looked down at the printed form the woman had given her. At first glance it looked like any other. Full name of child . . . date of birth . . . race . . . place of birth . . . full name of father . . . full maiden name of mother . . . She filled it in as she read, not pausing until she came to the words, "Purpose for which this copy is needed."

Robin's heart gave a little warning thump and she looked up sharply. The woman who had been waiting on her, however, had gone back to her desk to answer a ringing phone and was not watching her. After a moment's thought, she decided truth was the only answer and wrote in firmly, "Wish to discover true mother and father." The rest of the form was routine and she filled it in quickly, her excitement growing as she waited for the clerk to return.

PART THREE: *Francie*

Somewhere in one of those rows of neat and efficient-looking files that marched away for almost a quarter of a block across the room, there was a birth certificate for *her*. Just like Judy Hart's. She'd seen Judy's a hundred times because it was neatly pasted inside the front cover of Judy's "Baby Book." In the "olden days" when looking at such things was a favorite diversion, she'd not known what it was; had never given it a second thought. But now she knew. Every baby had to have one. Every man, rich or poor, had to know who he *was*.

The gray-haired woman returned to the counter. "I'm sorry to have kept you waiting," she said with a smile. "Now let me see what I can do for you."

The woman's expression did not change but she was looking at the form Robin had filled out much too long. "You're adopted?"

Robin nodded. For the first time she felt apprehension.

The clattering of the typewriters increased to a din. The woman's voice rose above it. "If you're looking for your *original* certificate of birth, I'm afraid that record is sealed. It would take a court order or permission from your adoptive parents to produce it."

Original certificate . . . court order . . . Not only were the words formidable and frightening, but the woman was looking at her queerly, too. "Do your parents . . . your adoptive parents . . . know about this?"

First Robin shook her head, then nodded affirmatively which did not make things better at all. She tried to struggle out of it, to regain her poise. "I don't understand. If . . . if I were an exchange student, like you said, and I had to have my birth certificate for travel purposes, wouldn't you have given it to me then?"

"Oh, there'd be no problem about that." The woman seemed almost grateful to be able to offer an explanation. "We have a birth certificate on file here that would be available to you on request. You see, a new one was made out for you at the time you were legally adopted. It would bear the names of your adoptive parents." She pointed to the form. "The names you've filled out here."

Robin could feel tears quivering behind her lids. She did not know whether it was less childish to let them show or to search in her purse for a handkerchief to wipe them away. To make matters worse, her hair was falling down. One large, tail-like piece had already escaped from her French roll and at any second the whole thing would collapse of its own weight.

"I'm sorry," the woman said, really looking sorry. "If you feel very strongly about it, perhaps when you're older . . . even now there might be other ways, but I'm sure it would be best for everyone to forget it for a while."

If she had not been sympathetic it would have been easier. Only the fiercest pride and the strongest will enabled Robin to stand straight, say thank you and leave with dignity. By the time she returned to the elevator and found her way out of the building, the exercise in control had given her an opportunity to appraise the situation more calmly. She had suffered a setback, not a defeat. Now she knew it had been foolishly optimistic to expect to find out a sixteen-year-old secret on the very first try.

And there might be other ways of going about it. Even the vital-statistic woman whose chief job seemed to be secret keeping, had intimated that. But whatever course she should take—and she still had more than half a day to take it in—the grown-up gambit was out. If she was going to find out who she was, she would have to look like herself while she did it. Using a shiny window of a parked car as a mirror, she took out the small arsenal of bobby pins, clips, hairpins, and combs that had been holding her hair in place, and combed it out so that except for her straight-cut bangs it fell like a sleek, shiny dark mane all around.

Turning from the window, she walked almost directly into the path of a young woman pushing a baby stroller. Too late she leapt out of the way. "Oh, pardon me! I guess I wasn't looking where I was going." She paused, even more embarrassed when she saw that something seemed to have happened to the front wheels of the stroller and that they no longer turned. "Golly, I hope I didn't make you do that when you had to stop so suddenly. Can I help someway?"

"You can give it a good kick, if you want," the mother replied. "But it's not your fault. The dumb thing. You just look crooked at it and the landing gear locks."

"Really? Kick it, I mean?"

"Right on the axle, or whatever that thing is that the wheels are fastened to. Just don't hurt your foot doing it."

Robin kicked, the young woman gave the stroller a smart backward jerk, then a push forward as the wheels began to turn.

The victors exchanged pleased looks.

"The prettiest baby!" Robin cried, giving the infant's fat hand a little pat. It was her final act of amendment before going on.

Actually, she thought, as she proceeded down the street that she had seldom seen such an un-pretty baby. It had a big, round pudding face with raisins for eyes and an absolutely expressionless expression. The prettiest baby, indeed! But its mother thought it beautiful. She had smiled and beamed in reply saying, "Say 'thank you,' Gwyneth. Say 'thank you for the compliment,'" as if pudding face were on the verge of speech instead of a bubble.

Then the idea struck. Robin almost laughed aloud. Prettiest baby, indeed! *She* had been the prettiest baby. At least, the prettiest baby they'd ever had at the Child Jesus Home.

"I'm afraid that if you don't have an appointment with Mrs. Heathcote you won't be able to see her. She's *very* busy."

"I'll wait," Robin said meekly. "If I may."

At this, the tall equine-looking woman who had answered Robin's knock looked, if possible, less pleased than she had before. She did, however, open the door wide enough for Robin to step inside.

"You may wait in the parlor. Through that door to your right. This was the old Leach mansion, you know," she added grudgingly, "before the Home acquired it. And a more inefficient, backbreaking, woman killer of a house you wouldn't find if you searched the state over. But it's ours, and we do with it the best we can." She let out a long, quivering neigh and once more affixed Robin with a stone-hard eye. "But because I'm letting you wait, mind, is no indication that you'll get to see Mrs. Heathcote today." She did not wait for an acknowledgement but charged off across the hall to another smaller room and shut the door.

A moment later she reappeared, dashed to the back of the house apparently to answer a ringing phone, came back and then clattered up the broad staircase giving Robin, in passing, a look that said, "See, we're *all* busy."

If it were not for the nervousness that had been building up in her ever since the collision with Gwyneth and her mother that triggered the decision to come back to the Home she had left as a baby sixteen years ago, she would have enjoyed her surroundings.

Something was happening every minute. A group of toddlers, shepherded by a grandmotherly-looking woman with rosy cheeks, returned from a walk. The doorbell rang. Miss Hustle-and-Bustle answered it and admitted a man wearing wash pants and a clean, blue work-shirt who said, "I'm Hedwig's fadder. My wife out of hospital now. I take Hedvig home, plees." His accent was thick and hard for Robin to understand. When he was invited into the parlor with her he only smiled and shook his head and stood waiting by the door until Miss H. and B. returned with a fat baby girl lolling back in a blue plastic infant seat.

Before the door closed behind them, there were voices on the stair. Three people were descending: a young woman carrying a tiny baby wrapped in a film of pink blanket, a young man with one arm held protectively about the woman, and a second woman with the most beautiful young-old face Robin had ever seen.

Safely at the foot of the stairs, the young couple paused. "We can never thank you." They had spoken almost in unison, one voice deep the other soft and feminine, each almost breaking with emotion.

Robin turned away. Tears she had not known were coming had splashed down on her purse that lay across her knees. She scrubbed them away with a piece of tissue then dabbed at her eyes. She was not alone in the room.

"Sadness and gladness both bring forth tears. It is strange," said the beautiful young-old woman Robin had seen on the stair. "We've placed hundreds of babies since I've been here, but it's a story that never grows old.

Each baby . . . each new mother and father. There's fresh wonder every time. I like my job so much that I'm not at all sure that I wouldn't pay just to work here. Even on a day like today. I expect Miss Beam has managed to let you know that we're not operating at the peak of our efficiency today. Our resident social worker is home with a bad cold and our best volunteer helper is in the hospital having a baby of her own. But thanks to Miss Beam, who has the gift of being in two places at the same time, we're managing. And, at least, she didn't send you away . . ." She paused with a bright, clear look and waited for Robin to begin.

On the long bus ride, from the State Office building to the Child Jesus Home, Robin had decided that a casual rather than a frontal approach would be best. "For personal reasons," she would say, "I would like to find out a little something about my mother."

Now she could not imagine saying that at all.

"Yes?" Mrs. Heathcote did not look at her wristwatch but the inflection of her voice would have denoted the passage of valuable time even if the peripatetic Miss Beam had not at that moment stuck her head in the parlor and whinnied, "Case workers meeting."

"I . . . that mother and father with the new baby. I . . . I came from here."

"Oh, how lovely of you to stop!" Mrs. Heathcote's cheeks glowed pinkly.

Robin shook her head. Her cheeks felt on fire. "That

isn't why I came. I mean, my reason is to find out who my mother is. To find out . . . who I am."

"Oh, please . . ." Mrs. Heathcote said. Her embarrassment seemed as acute as Robin's own. "We keep no records like that here. If we did, my own personal feelings would not permit . . ."

"I don't understand . . ." Robin mumbled the words without looking up.

"We don't *place* babies," Mrs. Heathcote said, gently. "We only care for them until the particular agency responsible for the baby chooses the adoptive parents. Usually we have a baby no more than a few days, though sometimes because of legal details it is longer before his new parents come and take him away. The other children here we care for only temporarily—until their own parents are in a position to care for them again. Only rarely does one of them become available for adoption."

"I see," Robin said. Really, she did not see at all. Everything was growing more confusing by the minute. "Would the agency that placed me . . ." She hated saying the words "agency" and "placement." They made her feel as if she were a human pawn on a gigantic chessboard that an unseen hand had moved around at will. ". . . if I found which agency it was that placed me, would someone there tell me . . . who I am?"

Mrs. Heathcote shook her head. "I'm afraid it would be the same story wherever you went. Without written permission from your parents, who I am sure love you very much, no one would disclose information that your natural mother most obviously did not wish to be known."

"But why?" Robin cried. She did not mind that Mrs. Heathcote could not help but see that tears filled her eyes. "Why would she want to keep it a secret, unless . . . she'd done something wrong?"

There was a horrible waiting silence broken by a commotion at the door as Miss Beam charged in dragging a vacuum sweeper and an armload of attachments. "Can't put off cleaning any longer in *here*," she said to Robin.

Mrs. Heathcote rose and gave Miss Beam a grateful glance. She pressed Robin's hand. "Give up your search, my dear. Go home . . ." The rest was lost in the sweeper's roar as Robin stumbled out.

3

Judy was sitting on the James' front step when Robin came up the walk. Robin had seen her from halfway down the block, forcing her to compose herself even more than the long brooding walk from the Child Jesus Home had done. Still, it was not enough.

When Judy, jumping up, demanded, "And where, may I ask, have you been until three o'clock in the afternoon? You can't have been job-hunting all this time?" it vanished in a short, almost hysterical outburst.

"Hush! Will you, please!" Robin waved frantically in the direction of the open windows of her house.

PART THREE: *Francie*

"Oh, don't have a fit, for Heaven's sake," Judy said, placidly. "Your mother's not home or I wouldn't have said it. I just got here a minute or two ago, myself. There's a note for you propped up against the sugar bowl in the kitchen—the door was open so I just walked in—saying she's gone off somewhere to photograph a chat. Whatever that is."

Robin brushed past Judy on her way into the dark, cool interior of the house. "It's a bird, stupid. One of mother's favorites. I'm not surprised that's she not here. Some Audubon person phoned yesterday to say a pair had been spotted in Pickett's thicket. I expect they've located its nest. It's the largest member of the warbler family," she added, as Judy continued to pad along behind her. "But unlike most of the other warblers it does not go farther north to nest..."

"You look as if you've been crying, too," Judy said in a penetrating tone.

Face to face with Judy in the bright, sunny kitchen Robin could not deny it.

"But not because you didn't get a job." It wasn't a question. Just a flat, Judy-statement. And there was no use to deny that either. Silently, Robin took a bottle of milk and a jar of homemade chocolate syrup from the refrigerator, put them on the table, got two glasses.

"You've been trying to find out something," Judy said. "I can tell just by looking at you."

"What if I have?" Under Judy's flat, diagnostic stare

Robin felt her temper begin to flare. It didn't help that part of her anger was directed at herself. "What's wrong with trying to find out who I am?" She shoved a glass of chocolate milk across the white formica table top toward Judy. "A lot of good it did me to try. Everywhere I went, I bumped into a stone wall."

Judy took a long swallow of milk then put down her glass. "You mean you really tried?"

Robin nodded. Not only had Judy's eyes been round with genuine surprise, but there had been such a note of grudging admiration in her voice that she could not help telling Judy everything. Her encounter with the woman in the department of vital statistics, the meeting with the woman with the baby, and finally, the futile interview with Mrs. Heathcote at the Child Jesus Home.

Judy stared into the murky pool of chocolate in the bottom of her glass. She looked a little shaken. "I still think it would be better for everybody if you forgot the whole thing, but it does seem that somewhere you should be able to find out. It's almost . . . well, it's almost a Civil Right to know who you are." She chewed thoughtfully at her lip. "The name of your real mother and father are probably on your adoption papers. They'd have to be. But they would be as hard to get hold of as your birth certificate. Harder, probably. Your dad would have them locked up in his safety deposit box at the bank." She sighed. "No doubt it's all for the best, even if I did get so excited I forgot what I came over here to find out. If you can stay all night. My folks are going out."

"Gee, Judy, I'd like to, but I don't think I ought to tonight." Robin forced regret she did not feel into her voice. "I promised Mother and Daddy I'd go somewhere with them tonight."

"Well, another time," Judy said so philosophically that Robin could not help wondering if she had known it was a lie.

It was an ordinary steel box, fourteen inches square, perhaps, and ten inches deep, painted black and with the name WILL JAMES painted in yellow on its side. A small brass padlock was slipped through the double loops that formed the fastening.

Her father thought it was hidden. Yet Robin could not remember how long—four years, perhaps even five—that she had known its hiding place.

Looking for it had been a game prompted by nothing more than a dinner table conversation long ago.

"A safety deposit box at the bank would be so much better, Will, than that old thing," her mother said.

"I know," her father said, a little foolishly. "It was my dad's. That's why I'm attached to it. Actually, there's nothing in it that anyone would want. Papers. And some non-negotiable bonds."

Her mother laughed in spite of herself. "I'm not asking you to give it to the Salvation Army or a rummage sale, Will, dear. Just to get a box at the bank. It would be so much more businesslike."

"Businesslike!" her father said with mock horror. "No one can accuse me of that!"

Then both of them had laughed for it was true.

"Still," he said, "I bet I can hide it where you will never find it," and after dinner he went upstairs and they heard him scratching around, walking back and forth. When he came back down a little later, he said, "There!" and looked both flushed and pleased.

Whether her mother had looked for the box after that, Robin did not know. But every time she was alone in the house *she* did. At last, when she had found it—it did not take a half dozen tries—she stared at it then as she did now.

The moment Judy was out of the house and wheeling down the street on her bike she had gone upstairs to her father's study and shut the door. The box was still hidden in the same place—just pushed to the back of a shelf in the bookcase with seldom-used books concealing it from view.

She stared at it guiltily. She had not seen it or thought about it since the day that searching she had found its hiding place. And today, if it had not been for Judy and her talk of adoption papers and safety deposit boxes she would not have thought about it now.

She reached out her hand, then withdrew it. Still, if the box were not locked it would be all right to look inside. Perhaps the padlock would spring open at her touch. Perhaps there was nothing in the box at all. Surely, it would do no harm to see.

It was heavier than she had thought it would be. And there was something inside. She pulled at the little padlock but it did not yield. Almost without thinking, she took a paper clip from her father's desk, straightened it and probed into the little opening at the bottom of the lock. But nothing happened, except for a little scratch the paper clip made on the metal. Still, this small thing seemed to bring her to her senses. Aghast, she looked down at her hands as if they did not belong to her; nor knew what they had been doing. Quickly, she replaced the box where she found it and left the room.

Laura James talked of nothing but her chat throughout dinner. Even now that dinner was over she could not quite give him up. "Such a beautiful male," she sighed.

"What about me?" her father asked, in a silly mood. His day at the laboratory had been eventful, too.

"You don't have a bright yellow coat," said Laura James. "*Or* a plain little wife. And this one was such a show-off. He just couldn't resist leading us to his nest."

"Now about my grasshoppers," her father said. "This fellow's coat was *green*..."

"Outside! Outside! The two of you," Robin said. "I'll clean up the kitchen."

"If you're sure you want to..."

"I do," Robin said, really meaning it. A warm little rush of affection poured over her as she watched them walking side by side across the grass. The sweet fragrance of evening came through the open window. Her father, home early, had changed into his gardening clothes and had done the mowing before dinner. He had really done it nicely this time, she thought, as she looked out at the sweet-smelling green sward. Once, last summer, when his power mower was new, he had absent-mindedly gone right through one of her mother's perennial borders. Her mother said that only a saint would forgive him. So she had.

The table was cleared, the dishes rinsed and stacked when the knock came at the front door.

"Eighty cents," said the pint-sized boy on the door step. "I'm Dave Brock, your new carrier salesman and I've come to collect."

In the growing twilight he reminded Robin of Cass's little brother, Louis. She felt a small stab of pain. She had been so occupied with her own problem that Cass, who had started it all, was now almost forgotten.

With difficulty, Robin erased the image of Cass's pale, strained face from her mind. She had not forgiven her.

"Just a minute," she told the boy. "I'll get some money from my dad."

Fireflies were glimmering palely in the dusk and her parents were but vague blurs at the far end of the garden when she went to the back door and called, "Paper boy!"

PART THREE: *Francie*

"My wallet's on the bureau in my bedroom," her father called back. "And give the kid an extra dime."

Robin turned on the overhead light in her parents' room. The wallet lay in a welter of objects. Loose coins, a ring of keys, a Kennedy half-dollar in a small plastic case, a pocketknife, a small, smooth stone that had attracted him somewhere that day on his rounds.

She took a dollar bill from the wallet, went back downstairs, and paid the boy. Then once again she returned to her parents' room. This time she did not turn on the light. Even in the now-darkness she did not need it. Without volition, but unerringly, her hand sought and found the ring of keys. She slipped them in the pocket of her denim jumper.

Only a moment later the back door slammed and she heard her parents come inside. She stood immobile. It was not too late to put the keys back where she had found them. It would do no harm, however, to keep them for a while. Possession of them had happened so suddenly, so fortuitously, that she needed time to think. If her father missed them, which would be unlikely at least before morning, he would think he was the one who had misplaced them. And she could drop them almost anywhere where he could find them.

She closed her cold hand around the keys to silence their tell-tale jangle and slowly went downstairs.

A little after ten o'clock her mother, tired from her day in the open air, went upstairs to bed. Shortly afterward, her father followed. They were still talking a few minutes later when Robin tapped at their bedroom door. "I'm going to watch the late movie on TV if the sound won't bother anyone."

"It won't bother me," her mother promised drowsily. "There's nothing like pursuing a chat all day to make one knit up the ravel'd sleeve of care."

"Nor bother me." Her father yawned noisily as if to prove his words.

"Sleep late in the morning, honey, if you can." There were murmured good-nights, then the strip of light beneath the door gave way to darkness.

Although she still had not made up her mind, Robin did not allow herself to think at all as she got undressed and ready for bed. The face that looked back at her, however, from the bathroom mirror was of a girl she did not know at all. Her eyes glittered so brightly and her color was so high she could not help but wonder if her mother and father had noticed.

Back downstairs, she turned on the television set and curled up in a big chair before it. She really did not watch, yet even without watching she knew it was a stupid movie. Stupid and unreal. Even so, she did not stir until the grandfather clock had struck the hour of midnight, then she turned off the set and went upstairs. No sound came from her parents' room and her feet were silent on the strip of hit and miss rag rug that carpeted the hall. The door to her father's study she had foresightedly opened earlier. The clicking sound it made as she closed it was almost inaudible. Her heart pounded as she turned on a small but powerful light that stood on the desk, moved the box from its hiding place and focused the beam upon it.

With an icy hand she reached into the pocket of her robe for the keys, held them, too, beneath the light. There were nine keys on the ring. Earlier in the evening she had examined them. Only two of the nine were small enough to consider a possibility. Fumblingly, she separated one from the other and stared at the box as if the intensity of her gaze might force it to yield its secret without an act of betrayal.

Had Pandora stood so before *her* box? Had her heart pounded like some wild thing against the cage of her chest before she untied the ropes that loosed a thousand evils into the world? Robin gave her head an impatient shake. Pandora was a mythical creature. She was a real girl. If the papers were in the box, she thought, it's meant for me to know. If they're not in the box, I'll never try again to find out who I am.

The first key she tried slipped so smoothly into the lock that she scarcely had time to think. And when, a moment later, at the gentlest pressure it sprang open in her hand she felt a numbness creep along her spine. She had done it. The box was open. It was filled almost to the brim with important looking papers. The numbness had now extended to her hand. As she lifted each paper out, one by one, they crackled importantly in the stillness.

Insurance policies, government bonds, her father's last

will and testament, another for her mother. At a sound behind her, Robin froze. But it was only the rising wind rustling the blind at a half-open window. The adoption papers were the last in the box. Important, legal-looking, officially stamped and embossed, she unfolded the impressive looking document with fingers she could not control. Her eyes traveled the first page but she seemed to be reading as if underwater. Herewith . . . thereby . . . thereunto . . . judicial words, her parents' familiar signatures blurred and distorted, waveringly swam toward her. Then she saw it. The name she had never seen before. Scrawled in a childish but legible hand *Francine E. Smith.* Beneath it was space for the signature of another parent but none was there.

4

The librarian, dressed all in black, leaned over the desk and with a disapproving look intoned, "The City Directories for the last sixteen years are sealed. We cannot let you see them without an order from the court." He picked up a black-swathed gavel, then let it fall. "Go home. The case is closed."

The dream had been so real, so frightening that even now in the sunshiny brightness of morning Robin could not help but be a little fearful as she approached the desk in the reference room of the big public library downtown.

The librarian, however, to whom Robin addressed her request, was young, pretty, and obliging. She did not seem to think it at all surprising that anyone should ask for a City Directory published sixteen years before. "If you just sit down," she said, "I'll have the page bring your book."

Still, Robin's heart beat erratically as she chose a table. When she thought of why she was here, she felt quite ill. When she thought of the night before she could scarcely believe that she had done what she had done. It was as if something outside her body had possessed her. Yet what she had done was no dream. She had stolen her father's keys, broken into his strong box, then after she had found what she was looking for she had returned the papers to the box, placed the box on the shelf, and crept back to bed.

But she had not gone back to bed to sleep. Francine Smith . . . Francine E. Smith . . . she whispered the name over and over as the questions hammered at her brain. Francine Smith was her name, but who was she? Who was the boy? And how had it happened? And where was Francine Smith now?

When morning came her mother had looked at her curiously. "I didn't hear you come to bed. You must have stayed up quite late."

"Oh, no," she lied. "I turned the television off at twelve." At least, that was the truth.

The page, a tall thin boy, approached silently, placed the book on the table before her and went away.

Robin fingered the book. It was big, unwieldy, fluffy-paged from years of use and bound in a dark, dirty-red. She opened it near the end, her fingers trembling as she reached the S's.

Why should she be so nervous? There would be a hundred Smiths or more. There was only the remotest chance that she would find the one that she was looking for. But if she did, what then?

Even in the small type in which the book was set, the name leaped up at her from the solid column of Smiths. Francine E., 1801 Bowser Street.

The words blurred on the page. When someone said "Robin," she looked up but seconds passed before she could see that it was Sam.

"Hey, you sick or something that you come to the library in the summer when there isn't any school?"

"There was something I wanted to look up," she mumbled. "Anyway, you're here."

"Yeah, I'm here," Sam said. He looked a bit flustered but he stood his ground. "If you're through doing whatever you're doing, I'll take you home. I've got a car. It's not fancy, but it's mine."

"I'm not through. I'm going to be here a pretty long time yet."

"I can wait. Just killing time anyway. My new job doesn't start until next week. Had to have the car for the job."

"Sam, please! I don't *want* you to wait, don't you understand?" Nervousness caused her voice to rise above the whisper in which she had been speaking and the little librarian looked up from her desk and shook her head.

"Well, if that's the way you feel," Sam said, without rancor. "That's the way you feel. See you."

Robin was so relieved to see him go that not until he was safely out the door did she feel a twinge of remorse. She was sorry not to have asked Sam either about his job or his car. But she could not have him hanging around wanting to know why she wanted to go, of all places, to 1801 Bowser Street.

Robin did not like the look of the neighborhood at all. She did not like the idea of Francine Smith living on Bowser Street. Not that she would still be living there. But seeing the house where she *had* lived, walking down the street she had walked could not help but bring Francine Smith out of the shadows; help make her real. She could not bring herself to say "help make her more my mother."

Robin shifted the library books she was carrying to her other arm. They were getting heavier by the minute but she had need of them. Back home, the books would be proof that she'd gone to the library, where she had told her mother she was going.

From the directions the traffic policeman near the library had given her, she had not thought she would have so far to walk. Twelve or fifteen blocks, he said. And she was used to walking almost that far to school each day.

But perhaps the blocks on Bowser Street were longer, she thought. Certainly, they were sadder. Not sad in the sense that the street Cass lived on was sad. There, remnants of former grandeur still remained. Great trees still stood. But it was hard to imagine these dilapidated houses, the dingy apartment buildings, small stores and shops ever being very comfortable or nice.

Signs "Rooms for Rent," "Vacancy," "Meals—Day, Week, or Month" were propped in front of grimy curtains in first floor windows. Even traffic was scant. A blue sedan and a black panel truck were the only cars in sight. Robin scuffed along. House numbers were growing smaller as she walked. She could not not be far from 1801. Yet when she reached the place on the block where it should be, she stopped with a sense of shock. There was nothing there at all. Only a few scattered, flaking bricks, a little heap of dusty plaster, a paper-thin red poppy, its green leaves grayed with dust, growing near three crumbling cement steps that led nowhere— these were the only evidences that a building had once stood there. A small, sudden gust of wind sent a scrap of old newspaper skittering toward her. It came to rest at her feet: "SUMMIT TALKS FAIL . . ."

She sat down on the steps that led nowhere, laid the books beside her. She squeezed her eyes tightly shut, feeling tears welling behind her lids, then gave her head an impatient shake. It was foolish to be disappointed. Stupid. Never in her wildest imaginings had she expected to find Francine Smith still living where she'd lived six-teen years before. And if she had been, "what then?" was a question she could not yet bring herself to answer.

"Looking for someone?" the old man said. He was small, stooped, and his eyes rheumy. A withered hand, bony as a bird's claw, clasped the knob of the walking stick he held before him on the sidewalk.

"I . . . I don't know. I mean, not really," Robin said. Two days had passed since her first visit to Bowser Street. She had not meant to come again. She had not wanted to. Yet, that afternoon when her mother went upstairs to see if she could nap away a headache, the "force" proved stronger. She left a note saying she would be back soon propped against the sugar bowl in the kitchen. And had come.

"They made the folks move out and tore the building down because they said the urban renewal was coming through," the old man said. He stared at the little pile of rubble as if in his mind the building still stood. "That was five years ago and it hasn't come through yet. Too bad for the folks that lived there. Some of 'em, though, still lives here and around."

"Was . . . was it an apartment?"

"Rooming house. Rooming house, at least for as long as I can remember."

"You didn't ever know a girl who lived there? A long time ago. A girl named Francine Smith?"

"Don't recall," the old man said. He sat down on one of the cement steps that led nowhere and raised his face, eyes closed, to the warmth of the sun and seemed to forget that she was there.

Robin walked on. The old man had said that some of the people who lived at 1801 were still in the neighborhood. Now that she was here it would do no harm to try.

"I'm trying to locate a Francine . . ." The door closed so swiftly that Robin felt a little rush of air against her face. But at most of the dozen or so other places she had stopped, she'd been allowed to finish her carefully phrased little question before the person shook her head and squeezed the door shut again. Only once had she been afraid, and that was when an aged troll answered the custodian's bell in an apartment house, and at her question shook his head and vanished silently down a basement stair.

And only once did she have the faintest clue. That was at the sad little cafe on the corner. If it had not been for the striped cat in the window gazing out at her with inscrutable slitted eyes she would not have gone in at all.

After the sunshine of the street, the interior of the cafe was as dim as a cave. It seemed little more than a dark corridor, really, with a long counter running along one side and a little scattering of tables at the rear. There were no customers. Only a thin man with a bald head perched on a stool behind the cash register. Robin stood diffidently in the doorway until he put down his newspaper and looked up.

"Pardon me," she began, "but I'm trying . . ."

"Come in, little lady. Come right on in. No need to stand out there on the hot street when it's so nice and cool in here at the Mariner's Cafe."

A little warning prickle ran along her spine, but it seemed absurd to honor it. She moved one step forward and spoke with all the firmness she could muster. "I'm trying to locate someone named Francine Smith. She used to live in this neighborhood a long time ago."

"Sorry, little lady." The bald man shook his head. "The old owner might have helped you. He knew every man, woman and child on Bowser Street. But he sold out and went to L.A. a month ago. I'm the new owner."

"Well, thank you, anyway." She could not keep the disappointment from her voice.

"Hold on, hold on!" The bald man got down from his stool. "Wait'll I ask Charlie. He knew almost as many folks around here as the old man."

As if summoned by mental telegraphy, the swinging door at the rear of the cafe swung open and a wizened-looking little man, with a soiled dish-towel tied around his middle, came limping toward them.

"Ever hear of anybody by the name of . . . what's that again?"

"Francine Smith."

PART THREE: *Francie*

"Francine Smith," the bald man said as if Robin's voice had not been heard.

The wizened little man shook his head. "Sorry, miss." He had started back toward the kitchen when he turned. "Might they have called her *Francie?*"

"Francie . . ." Robin's stiff lips formed the name. "Maybe . . . I don't know . . ."

"If you mean Francie Smith, I remember *her*. She was a regular customer. Nice as they come, that kid. Then she dropped out of sight."

Robin felt a wave of faintness come over. As it receded she was aware of a stiff breeze. The bald man was fanning her with his newspaper. The wizened one thrust a glass of ice water in her hand. "Sure you're all right? Looked there for a minute that you might keel over. Don't you think you'd better sit down and rest yourself a while?"

She accepted the ice water, drained the glass, but refused the offer to sit down. After thanking them again she walked quite steadily out the door.

Although the faintness did not come again it was replaced by something that made her feel almost as ill. Her own wrongdoing had been the cause of it all. In tampering with the lives of others she had let loose a Pandora's box of troubles and gained nothing. Worse, she had lost much of what she had. She found a tired piece of tissue in her purse and wiped her drippy eyes. Only in Pandora's box, hope remained. In hers there was no hope at all. In her mind, as long as she lived, she would see Bowser Street as it looked in the listless heat of the June afternoon. The children that she had seen earlier had all disappeared. The black panel truck was parked beneath a dusty cottonwood tree half way down the block. The only thing that seemed to move, to have a life of its own was a paper-thin red poppy blooming in a weedy flower garden that bordered the front walk of the house she had just passed.

"A red poppy." Robin whispered the words. Perhaps her Pandora's box was not empty after all. She retraced her footsteps, went up the walk of the house where the poppy bloomed and rang the bell.

"I'm sorry, but I'm not interested," the woman with her hair done up in rollers said.

"I'm not selling anything, I just wanted . . ."

"That's what they all say. They say they're not selling anything, but . . ."

"Please, I'm trying to locate . . ."

"Who is it, Mildred?" The thin and reedy voice of an old woman came from inside the house.

"Just a girl, mother," the woman said, tiredly. "And I don't know what she wants. Trying to locate somebody, I guess."

"Let me talk to her, Mildred. It will help to pass the time."

The woman in curlers made a helpless gesture. "She's got a bad heart and we're supposed to keep her quiet, but what can you do? After they tore down her rooming house I had to come back to this miserable place to take care of her, but do you suppose I could get her to taper off? Not Mother! Oh, no, indeed! Even after she had her heart attack, what does she do the first day I go off to leave her alone for an hour. She goes out and plants a flower bed!"

"Was . . . was her rooming house at . . . 1801?"

"Why, yes," the woman said. "But how would you have known?" She gave Robin a close, suspicious look then led the way down a dark and musty hall.

The sunlight filtering through the dark green blinds gave the bedroom an eerie underwater cast. Robin's voice sounded hollow to her ears. "I'm trying to locate someone who lived at 1801 Bowser Street . . . a long time ago. Her name was Francine Smith."

There was neither answer nor movement from the big four-poster bed. Robin turned to go. Her hope had been so short-lived, despair had not yet had time to take its place. She could not expect anyone so old and ill as the hunched gray woman propped up against the pillows to remember.

"People who knew her, called her *Francie*," the old voice said, dryly. "But after all these years, there can be no harm in telling you what I know. Sit down. Sit where I can see you."

"I'll stand," Robin said in the voice of someone else. The hand that gripped the corner of the bed was too cold to be her own.

"Where she came from, I don't know. She didn't say.

I didn't ask. Lots of people who come to Bowser Street, then as now, have a secret that they keep. But there was a softness in her speech that folks who grow up in our part of the country do not have.

"Kids were wild for her. They'd come running when they saw her coming home from work, but it was the baby who lived next door she couldn't leave alone. 'My little girl would be just about her age,' she told me once, then added as if she needed to explain, that she'd given her baby away when she was born so she'd have a better life than she had had. I said the only thing I could—that she'd marry and have another little girl. I didn't know then that was not the thing to say. Not 'til later did I learn that she couldn't have another child."

The old woman stared across the room as if into the abyss of time. Robin's heartbeat slowed, came almost to a stop before the dry old voice resumed.

"She got sick not too long after that. Almost from the beginning I knew she couldn't go on alone. I guess she knew it, too. An uncle, a grim-faced man dressed like an undertaker, came to take her back to wherever it was she came from. Later, he forwarded a letter that she'd written me just before she died."

The old woman did not seem to hear Robin's sharp, indrawn cry. "I guess you don't get well," she said, "unless you try."

"And you don't get well if you spend all your strength and energy talking to strangers, either." The daughter's querulous voice came from the doorway.

PART THREE: *Francie*

Robin silently pressed a thank-you on the old gray hand on the coverlet, then walked down the halls and out doors.

The black panel truck that she'd seen twice before on Bowser Street was parked in front of the house. The door swung open as she neared and Sam said, "Get in."

5

Sam hunched over the wheel, looked straight ahead as the car moved down the street. "I'm here because your mother kind of asked me to look out for you. Not to spy. Just to be around in case you needed anything. Like today. You look pretty green around the gills."

"I . . . I'm all right." She stared down at her shoes, scuffed and dirty from walking. "She . . . they . . . knew?'

"Guessed," Sam said. He flushed and his jaws came shut in a way they had when he was through talking for a while.

"That's why you were at the library that day," Robin said slowly. "And every time I've come to Bowser Street, you've been here, too."

Sam did not answer. But there was no need. The circle was closing. Robin pressed her hands to her eyes. As hard as the day had been, there was one more thing that she must do. The ghost of Francie Smith would not rest easily until she and Cass, who needed friends, were friends again.

"You're here to see ..."

"Cass Carter," Robin said. "I've been here before."

"Oh, yes," the woman at the switchboard said with a smile. "Matron is out right now, but I'm sure it will be all right. Down the hall to your left, the south parlor where you talked before. But you'd best wait a minute until I call."

This time Cass was waiting. She got up from the chair, paused uncertainly, then flung herself into Robin's outstretched arms.

"I'm sorry!"

"I'm sorry!"

"I was hateful and mean ... I wanted to hurt you ..."

"But I should have understood. Besides, what you said was true. About me, I mean. About ... my mother."

Cass's eyes filled with tears. "I didn't know. Believe me. And it might not be true, what I said. Babies who are adopted aren't always illegitimate." She held on to

Robin's hand as if it were a life raft in a stormy sea. "Sometimes . . . sometimes they have fathers who want them."

"Mine didn't," Robin said flatly. It didn't hurt as much to say it as she had thought it would. Her shoulders straightened. "I've another father now, who does. And another mother. Because my first mother wanted me to have a better life than she had had. I found that out since the day that I was here. She . . . my mother died a long time ago."

The silence in the room was broken by a frightened whisper. "Cass, it's *him!*" The girl, dressed in skirt and smock, who stood in the doorway, was wide-eyed with alarm. "Miss Wheat, at the switchboard, asked me to tell you. M . . . Matron isn't here. What are you going to do?"

Two rounds of color burned in the whiteness of Cass's face. "I don't have to see him. I won't see him. There's nothing he can want of me now."

"*I* saw him," said the other. She giggled self-consciously. "He's cute enough all right. If he was my fellow, I'd see him all right."

"You see him, then," Cass answered. Color was glowing even higher in her cheeks. "*I'm* not going to be bought off by his father's money, like I was a piece of livestock, to ease his conscience . . . And I'm not going to be shipped out of town so they don't have to be reminded of me. After almost a month, I can't think of any other reason why he'd come."

She turned to Robin who stood in stricken silence. "Unless . . . unless that's the reason I *should* see him. To tell him to his face! Yes, I think I should like that!" She whirled toward the openmouthed girl still standing in the door. "I've changed my mind, after all. You can tell Mr. Brewster Bailey Winfield, the Third, that Cass Carter the First will see him in Parlor B."

Cass had only time to say, "Do I look all right?" and Robin time to answer with a quavering but honest "You look beautiful" before Brew was there, his bulk filling the doorway.

"Hi, Cass. It's me." Brew's voice was a mixture of little boy bravado and feigned good cheer.

Cass did not answer but stood straight and regal as a queen. Her eyes flashed imperiously. Her burnished copper-colored hair burned bonfire bright in the small drab room.

Robin, who had shrunk into the nearest corner at Brew's entrance, felt a shiver run along her spine. "D . . . don't mind me. I'm just going." She started edging toward the door.

"Why go?" said Cass. Her voice was wire-tight and controlled. "There's no need to go rushing off. There isn't anything that Brew has to say to me that he can't say in front of you. That's right, isn't it, Brew?"

A dark red flush stained Brew's face. "I don't know about that. I hoped, I mean, you and I've got things to talk about. I don't think a third person ought to be here."

"That's interesting! *I* think a third person is the very thing we need. Robin can be a witness. After all, you've come with a business proposition. So why don't we just get down to business. I'd like to hear what it is. Hear just how much it's worth to the great Brewster Bailey Winfield and his family to forget I ever lived."

"It wasn't that I came about," Brew said. He looked so embarrassed, so miserable that Robin could almost feel a shred of pity.

"I . . . I don't understand," Cass said. Her nervous fingers working against the palms of her hands made a dry whispering sound. The little rounds of color in her cheeks had disappeared.

"I've been thinking . . ." Brew cast an anguished glance at Robin who, once again, was too mesmerized to move. "I . . . I've been thinking about the kid. He might be an athlete, like me. Only better. Greater. A champ. I could train him, see . . . from the time he was little . . ."

"And what about me?" Cass said. Her lips barely seemed to move. "Where do I fit in?"

Brew looked startled. "Why, we'd get married! That's why I came. My dad can't stop us. He doesn't even know I came to see you. And once the kid is here . . . once he sees it's a boy, he'll soften up. You'll see. Besides, I like you. I . . . I don't date Pris Gosling any more."

He paused with a nervous laugh and when Cass did not respond, took a shuffling step in her direction and mumbled on. "I guess I did act pretty rotten that night you told me. But I wasn't expecting you . . . I mean, I didn't think this was going to happen, see? And my folks started carrying on. They'd made plans for me. Big plans. You understand that, don't you, Cass?"

"Get out!" Cass spat out the words so fiercely that Brew stepped backward and held up his arm as if for protection.

"No need to get sore. We don't have to stay married. People get divorces all the time. But I could still see the kid. I wouldn't lose track of him. He . . . he'd be mine."

"*Your* kid? Don't make me laugh!" Cass said. Her bitter, caroling laugh shattered the silence of the room, then from somewhere the control that she had so briefly lost returned. "He's not going to be your kid, Brew," she said, softly. "And he's not going to be my kid, either. He's going to be the kid of somebody who gets married to stay married. Somebody who'll love him whether he's a great athlete or not . . ." A secret smile tipped the corners of Cass's mouth. ". . . somebody who'll love him, even if he turns out to be a girl—a girl like me."

Robin edged out the door and down the hall.

Sam was waiting. Robin lay her head back against the seat and closed her eyes. Tears, warm and cleansing, ran down her cheeks. Tears of sadness for Francie Smith whose life was over; for Cass Carter whose new life had just begun; tears of relief that her own foolish quest was finished; of happiness that her always-mother's and always-father's love remained; and last of all, tears of gladness for a friend like Sam.

The handkerchief he gave her was surprisingly clean. Gratefully, she wiped the tears away and as sparingly as possible blew her nose. And Sam, though silent, was smiling as the black panel truck bounced out the driveway of the Mission Hospital and turned toward home.

THE AUTHOR

Jeannette Eyerly has established a reputation as a writer who tackles the delicate situations and difficult problems faced by today's teen-agers. She is a pioneer in exploring such subjects as unwed motherhood, school drop-outs, mental illness, and the problems confronting children of divorced or alcoholic parents. She was presented with a 1969 Christopher Award for her novel about the use of drugs, *Escape from Nowhere*. Mrs. Eyerly was graduated from the State University of Iowa with a degree in English and journalism, has taught creative writing, and has contributed to major national magazines. She has lived in the same house in Des Moines for twenty-five years and has several grandchildren she brags about. She enjoys cooking, gardening, bird watching, and collecting art with her husband.